Tara

Beach Brides Series

by

Ginny Baird

Tara

Beach Brides Series

by

Ginny Baird

Published by

Winter Wedding Press

Copyright © 2017 Ginny Baird

Print Edition

ISBN 978-1-942058-24-3

Edited by Sally Knapp

Cover Design by Raine English

Elusive Dreams Designs

http://www.ElusiveDreamsDesigns.com

Introduction

GRAB YOUR BEACH hat and a towel and prepare for a
brand new series brought to you by twelve *New York
Times* and *USA Today* bestselling authors...

Beach Brides! Fun in the summer sun!

**Twelve heartwarming, sweet novellas
linked by a unifying theme. You'll want to read
each one!**

BEACH BRIDES SERIES (Tara)

Twelve friends from the online group, Romantic
Hearts Book Club, decide to finally meet in person
during a destination Caribbean vacation to beautiful
Enchanted Island. While of different ages and stages in
life, these ladies have two things in common: 1) they
are diehard romantics, and 2) they've been let down by
love. As a wildly silly dare during her last night on the

island, each heroine decides to stuff a note in a bottle addressed to her "dream hero" and cast it out to sea! Sending a message in a bottle can't be any crazier than online or cell phone dating, or posting personal ads! And, who knows? One of these mysterious missives might actually lead to love...

Join Meg, Tara, Nina, Clair, Jenny, Lisa, Hope, Kim, Rose, Lily, Faith, and Amy, as they embark on the challenge of a lifetime: risking their hearts to accomplish their dreams.

This is Tara's story....

A Savannah billionaire finds a message in a bottle on the beach when he's about to propose to his socialite girlfriend, and his whole life turns on a dime.

Meet the Beach Brides!

MEG (Julie Jarnagin)
TARA (Ginny Baird)
NINA (Stacey Joy Netzel)
CLAIR (Grace Greene)
JENNY (Melissa McClone)
LISA (Denise Devine)

HOPE (Aileen Fish)
KIM (Magdalena Scott)
ROSE (Shanna Hatfield)
LILY (Ciara Knight)
FAITH (Helen Scott Taylor)
AMY (Raine English)

Prologue

TARA'S MESSAGE IN a bottle...

SOS!
Mend my broken heart.

If you're smart,
If you're sexy,
If you dare...

IrishLass@...

Chapter One

HEATH WELLINGTON PATTED the pocket of his tuxedo jacket, finding the ring box wedged securely in place. He'd decided to bite the bullet and ask Caroline Chesterfield to marry him. They walked along the deserted Georgia shore, admiring the distant horizon. The grenadine sun was emerging, seemingly rising out of rollicking waves on this balmy October morning. The Caribbean storm that had assaulted the area had nipped at the coastline farther south, but it had fortunately spared Savannah. The genteel southern town wasn't always so lucky, particularly during hurricane season.

Heath had his pants legs rolled up and Caroline clutched at the hemline of her long green sequined dress, lifting it above the surf. They'd both left their shoes back by the pier and now strode barefoot along the gritty sand, as minute pieces of broken shell prickled their toes and poked at their insteps. The water temperature was tepid, its lingering warmth caused by months of unbearable summer heat. Yet cool pockets swirled in eddies, brought in with the tide from the chillier depths of the encroaching sea. Cockle shells were scattered about, as were moon snails and the occasional hollowed whelk. Colorful olive shells with various spiraling patterns dotted the broad beach, glistening with specks of seawater that shone like morning dew.

Caroline paused to rescue a sand dollar that had been trapped in a nest of seaweed. It was perfectly formed and elegant. Just like Caroline, in her stylish halter dress with her blond hair twisted tastefully in a loose chignon above her nape. Tendrils spilled forth and a section of her hair had become undone, in part thanks to the rippling breeze, but also as a testament to a night of vigorous dancing. Their couple friends Byron and Sara had tied the knot yesterday evening, with Sara's well-heeled parents hosting a blowout reception afterwards. Both Heath and Caroline had been wedding attendants. She'd been a bridesmaid while Heath had served as Byron's best man.

"It's beautiful!" Caroline picked up the sand dollar, handing it to him. Heath accepted it with an open palm, admitting to himself that Caroline was, too.

He smiled back at her and her deep blue eyes sparkled. "Just like you."

He should do it. *Just do it.* This was the ideal opening, right here. Right now. Out on spectacular Tybee Island.

Another couple approached, walking toward them. The man and woman were also in formal attire, but there was something different about them. They were laughing with each other, sharing some kind of private joke, as they happily ambled along hand in hand. Heath wasn't sure why, but he and Caroline rarely held hands. Not that this form of PDA was really necessary. There were clearly other things that mattered more.

Color warmed Caroline's cheeks. "You're such a talker," she said, referring to his previous compliment. "Ultra smooth." She retrieved the sand dollar from his hand and gently set it down in the sand, leaving it for a shell collector. While Caroline routinely spotted treasures on the beach, she rarely saved them.

"Smoothness pays with what I do," Heath commented, as they moved along.

"Sure does." She managed a saucy laugh. "Pays big-time, *Billionaire Banker.*"

Heath inwardly bristled at the new nickname she'd bestowed on him. While, professionally, he was pleased with his latest merger, he didn't spend inordinate amounts of time reflecting on how it impacted his personal bottom line. Heath was good at what he did, but his focus wasn't purely monetary. It was on the viability of his bank, as that affected the livelihood of the people who worked there. His Granddad Lyle had begun the business years ago, and it had grown from a simple savings and loan to an important international institution, with affiliates overseas and corporate offices in major U.S. cities.

"True," he answered mildly. "But there is more to life than that." Heath patted his jacket pocket again, gathering his nerve. He'd talked this through with Byron before the wedding, and understood that Byron was right. At thirty-six years old, Heath was unlikely to find the idealized version of a female he had in mind. Who could be more *ideal* than Caroline? She was smart, gorgeous, and independently wealthy, which meant she wasn't after his money. A very important point to consider, according to Byron, who had a fortune of his own to protect.

Heath stopped walking and raked a hand through his wavy dark hair. "Caroline," he began, heaving a breath. His pulse raced and his palms felt clammy. But they'd been talking about this for *months*. Skirting around the edges. Hinting at the future. At least, *she* had been hinting. *A lot.*

"Are you all right?" Caroline touched his sleeve. "You seem a little winded."

"Uh—yeah, fine." Sweat beaded his hairline and dribbled down his neck beneath his starched collar. He loosened his bowtie a notch. "I was just thinking that maybe you and I—?" He tried. Heath really tried, but the words got clogged in his throat.

She viewed him hopefully, her delicate brow crinkling. "Yes?"

"We've been going out for a long time now."

Caroline nodded. "Nearly three years."

"And in all that time...we..." Heath swallowed hard. "We've been to a bunch of weddings."

Her lips twisted in consternation. "And?"

"*And...* We've done other things, too! Tons of things together... We've come to know each other pretty well, wouldn't you say? We've formed a special...allegiance."

Caroline folded her arms, and Heath had the sinking sensation this wasn't going well. "An allegiance?"

Heath knew what he was expected to say next: that he'd fallen desperately in love with her. Instead of that, he opted for something closer to the truth. "What I mean is, I've developed a particular...fondness for—"

"A fondness? I see." Her face clouded over. "Just what are you trying to tell me, Heath?"

He dug into his coat pocket, figuring it was now or never. From the way things had been going, they could only get better. Perhaps a flawless one-and-a-half-carat diamond would help lighten Caroline's mood?

Everything that had occurred between them over these past three years had been guiding them in this direction, steering Heath and Caroline down this primrose garden path. It was time. Past time, more than likely... Caroline was nearly Heath's age, and neither of them was getting any younger.

"Caroline, will you—?" His fingers tightened around the ring box just as she glanced over his shoulder.

"What's *that*?" she asked, pointing past him.

Heath pivoted toward the ocean's panorama, his gaze landing on the object in Caroline's sights. A lean vessel with darkly tinted glass and a frayed amber label bobbed up and down, darting in and out of the waves. "It looks like a bottle," he said, dropping his hand to his side. He trudged through the shallows, saltwater lapping against his rolled-up pants legs and soaking them through to the knees.

He reached for the item and scooped it off the undulating surface of the water. "It's a Chianti!" he proclaimed, amazed.

Caroline viewed him, perplexed. "Italian wine?"

Heath held up the bottle, examining it in the spreading sunlight. "No, the wine's all gone." He squinted at its contents and tilted the bottle sideways: a small scroll of paper knocked against the glass. "There's something else in here."

He carried it back to her and she gently took the bottle, spinning it slowly around in her hands. "Do you think it's a note?"

"Yeah. Weird." But in a cool kind of way, there was no denying that.

"Who would do that?" Caroline asked. "Send a message in a bottle? Must be some kind of joke."

"Or, an experiment, maybe?"

"It certainly can't be for real," Caroline decided. She bent down to wedge the bottle into the sand then dismissively wiped off her hands, dusting her palms together. "Now," she said, setting her hands on her hips. When she dropped the hem of her dress, it danced and billowed in the waves. "Wasn't there something you were about to tell—or ask—me?" Her lips tipped up in a grin and Heath's heart caught in his throat.

Incredibly, the episode with the bottle seemed to have turned Caroline's spirits around. Where before she'd appeared perturbed with him, at present she seemed resigned. Resigned and maybe even a tiny bit giddy, speculating about what might happen next. "Come on, Heath!" she challenged with a chuckle. "What were you going to *say*?" Her voice held an anticipatory edge, like she could already guess. And, she was guessing with uncanny accuracy.

The only trouble was...Heath was starting to wonder if he'd changed his mind. Marriage was an awfully big step; it wasn't something one rushed into, or undertook casually. Perhaps Heath needed more time to think on it—and feel ready? Wasn't that only fair—to Caroline, and to himself?

It occurred to Heath that a bad marriage would be worse than no marriage at all. He could wake up one morning with Caroline beside him, yet find himself utterly alone. Trapped with the wrong person for eternity. Marooned in unholy matrimony... His gaze roved over the bottle, stuck in the sand beside

Caroline's feet, and something inside him hitched. His heart jolted, and then it slammed harder, thundering fiercely again and again.

Heath felt like a man on the brink who'd just been pulled back from a ledge. What had he been thinking? He couldn't marry Caroline! Maybe he wasn't destined to marry anyone—ever. Because, if Heath knew anything clearly, it was that *fondness* wasn't enough. He wrenched the bottle out of the sand, securing it in his grasp. Then he headed for the pier with long, brisk strides. Caroline scurried after him, kicking up sand and spray as she went.

"Wait! Where are you going?"

"I'm sorry, Caroline. I think we've made a mistake."

"We?" The hurt in her voice rose above the wind.

Heath turned toward her and his shoulders sagged. "Me, it was me. My fault, and I'm sorry."

She stared at him, befuddled and dismayed. "Was it something I did?"

"No, you've been wonderful," he said hoarsely.

"Just not wonderful enough, huh?" A tear glistened in her eye and Heath felt like the earth's most colossal heel.

"Let me drive you home."

"Then what?"

Heath glanced at the bottle in his hand, having absolutely no idea. He only knew he needed space. And time to sort things out. "I'm afraid I don't know."

Her chin trembled. "You might not, but I do." Caroline stormed heatedly toward his car, grabbing her shoes along the way. Then she got in and slammed shut the door.

Heath nabbed his shoes from beside the pier and climbed into the driver's seat beside her. For a long while they both stared silently at the ocean. The tension was so thick between them they could hear gulls calling from several miles away. He didn't know whether her next barb was said just to wound him, or whether it was spoken in truth. "There's already somebody else, anyway."

did your job." Inside the bottle, the scrolled-up missive leaned sideways. On closer inspection, Heath noticed it was bound together with a small piece of string.

His eyes darted to the needle-nose pliers he'd withdrawn from his toolbox earlier and placed on the table. Heath intended to use those to carefully extract the note from the bottle, in case it didn't easily spill out once he'd uncorked it. He considered the bottle a moment more before pressing his thumbs against the cork. *Son of a gun, it's wedged in tight.* He tried again from another angle, then nabbed a dishtowel from nearby and tugged. The person who'd driven this cork in must have used a sledgehammer!

Heath stood and strode to a kitchen drawer, extracting his trusty corkscrew. The high-end apparatus never failed him, and it made easy work of the reticent Chianti cork. It popped loudly, its din resonating throughout the kitchen. Heath grinned, eagerly anticipating what the note might say. Hopefully it was written in jest, like Caroline surmised. Heath certainly hoped a person wasn't legitimately shipwrecked somewhere. If this was a true cry for help, he'd have to bring it to the attention of the Coast Guard.

He leaned forward in his chair and carefully tipped the bottle upside down over the table. The rolled-up note slid toward the bottle's neck then became stuck at a weird angle. "Needle-nose pliers to the rescue," Heath proclaimed, picking up the instrument and gingerly plucking at one side of the little scroll.

It took a few different maneuvers, but Heath finally pinched together the top edges of the scroll, compressing them just enough so he could...very slowly...withdraw it. Aha! The head was born! And then—*whoosh!* The rest of the scroll slid out gracefully, its string only snagging for a brief moment against the narrow bottle lip.

"Well, here's the moment of truth," he said to the ring box as if it could answer. Then he slipped off the narrow piece of twine and unrolled the paper.

Heath flattened the wrinkled page out on the table and read the contents. As he did, his heart skipped a beat.

SOS!
Mend my broken heart.

If you're smart,
If you're sexy,
If you dare...

IrishLass@...

Heath glanced again at the glistening solitaire on the table, finding it impossible to believe that just hours ago he'd been prepared to ask Caroline to marry him. Caroline had never *dared* Heath to do anything. She'd never pushed—or challenged—him. In all their time together, Heath had convinced himself that was a good thing.

But if playing it safe was so wonderful, why then did Heath's pulse pound harder as he tried to fathom who had written this note? Was *she* smart? Was *she* sexy? Did she live in Ireland? This Irish Lass certainly seemed adventuresome, whoever—and wherever—she was.

Yet the most telling thing about her message was the earnestness of her admission. Irish Lass hadn't pretended to be brave or invincible. On the contrary, she'd shared a very personal truth. Some unworthy cad had broken her heart.

Heath viewed her exquisite penmanship, thinking she must have taken care with this note. It was deceptively short, yet the emotions behind it ran deep. Perhaps she'd been at her wit's end, and had given up. Maybe she'd just needed someone to talk to, yet nobody had been there...except this old Chianti bottle.

Heath's gaze returned to the bottle as he considered it anew. "Just where in the world did you come from?" He'd probably never know. The mystery of this message in a bottle was bound to remain unsolved.

Unless...he tried e-mailing her...

Heath pushed back in his chair, shaking his head at the crazy idea. What would he say? *Hey, I found your SOS?* This bottle could have been bobbing around in the Atlantic for years!

Well, okay, Heath conceded, probably not too many, given that the vintage of the wine was just six years old. That could mean that it was tossed soon after that particular batch of wine was bottled, or anytime between then and now. But if the bottle had traveled from Europe, it had to have been afloat for a while.

That would have to mean that Irish Lass had tossed it into the sea some time ago. She could already be married! Or at least engaged... It was also possible she'd forgiven the cad who'd broken her heart and they were living in wedded bliss with a baby in Dublin.

Heath heaved a breath, deciding he was reading too much into a simple note. He'd had a long day and hadn't slept at all last night. He was tired, overwrought, and probably a little thrown off base by his sudden breakup with Caroline. Not that he regretted it entirely, though he did hate the fact that he'd hurt her feelings.

He picked up the note again, noticing it was written on a small piece of stationery. It appeared to be from a notepad, the sort stocked beside telephones in hotel rooms. The name of a Caribbean resort was embossed in gold letters at the top of the page.

Had Irish Lass taken the notepad home before tossing her missive out to sea in Ireland? Or, had she actually been staying on this island when she'd made her move? Heath considered the name of the place, thinking he'd never heard anything about it. Then again, there were so many remote islands in that part of the world, some of them privately owned and home to exclusive resorts.

For an instant he had the impulse to research the place on the Internet and phone the front desk. Yeah, right. And what would he say? Heath clearly couldn't inquire about a brokenhearted Irish Lass who'd been a guest. Even if the hotel could, by some wild miracle, identify her, they'd surely keep her identity confidential.

Heath sighed and ran a hand through his hair, deciding there was nothing more to be done. He rolled up the note and secured it carefully with its twine before returning it to the bottle and very gently inserting the cork.

His historic townhome was just a short block away from Forsyth Park in downtown Savannah and it was a pleasant evening out. He'd take a stroll and a have an early dinner at one of his favorite restaurants nearby before calling it a day. Perhaps, if they had it on the menu, he'd order a special bottle of Chianti to accompany his meal.

Chapter Three

TARA MCADAMS REFILLED Jeannie's glass with the flavorful libation. She, and her best friend since the ninth grade, sat in a quaint Italian restaurant twenty miles from her hometown, which had no eateries of its own to speak of. Other than the places that sold fish. This part of Maine on Beaumont Bay and near Cadillac Mountain was known for its lobster, but every once in a while a girl needed her pasta.

"Say, isn't this the same kind of Chianti?" Jeannie asked, indicating the bottle.

"The one from Enchanted Island?" Tara savored her swallow of wine, considering what a foolish act that had been. Not that she'd really believed it would amount to anything at the time. "Yeah."

"Still nothing doing?"

Tara shrugged and set down her wineglass. "What could you really expect?"

"Well, I don't know about *you*." Jeannie gave a mischievous giggle. "But I was kind of hoping you'd hear from your Prince Charming, or something."

"I guess there's nobody that daring out there anymore."

Jeannie leaned forward and her dirty blond hair grazed her shoulders. "Or that *smart* and *sexy*," she said in a whisper.

Tara wryly twisted her lips. "If he's out there, he must be hiding."

Jeannie's gray eyes rounded. "Or married," she said in low tones. "Maybe that's the hold up?"

Tara hadn't even considered this, that she could have unwittingly become a home-wrecker. "That would be horrible," Tara hissed back. "Surely, a married man wouldn't respond?"

"An engaged one might," Jeannie commented.

"That's nearly as bad."

"I guess that depends on his fiancée," Jeannie returned and Tara swatted her with her linen napkin.

"It's never too late until you say *I do*, Tara." Jeannie contemplated her wineglass a moment then took a sip. "Maybe it's still floating out there—your bottle? Could be anywhere by now, you know?"

More than likely at the bottom of the ocean, Tara thought glumly. Who had she been fooling, thinking her desperate, far-flung measure might actually lead to something? She viewed the rustling autumn leaves through the restaurant window, as they turned orange and gold in the fading daylight. "It's been over four months, now. Who knows if it will ever be found? And, if it is...?" Tara sighed heavily. "What are the odds of him being all those things I asked for?"

Jeannie grimaced sympathetically. "Might not even be a *him*. A woman could discover the bottle."

"I've thought of that, too." Tara twisted her thick dark hair into a coil and brought it forward over one shoulder. "I just wish..."

"I know that you do," Jeannie said kindly.

"Pasta carbonara!" their waiter announced, appearing. He served Tara first then addressed Jeannie, setting down her plate. "And a garden lasagna for you." Delicious aromas drifted from both of the steaming entrees.

After their waiter departed, Jeannie said, "That must have been fun, being on that island with your online friends." She sounded a bit wistful, almost like she'd wanted to join them.

"Yeah, it was great. Fun to finally meet everyone in person."

"Has anyone else heard anything?"

"Meg met a television producer!" Tara said brightly.

"Yeah?"

"Yeah! He was filming on Enchanted Island when her bottle washed up."

"No way."

"Way. It got stuck on the shoals or something and got carried back in with the tide. I hear they're getting married."

Jeannie sighed dreamily. "Well, I guess that's one happy ending."

Tara raised her wineglass. "Here's to happy endings!"

Jeannie clinked her glass, then mysteriously said, "Speaking of that..." In one deft move, she withdrew the left hand she'd cagily concealed under the table. A new diamond sparkled on her ring finger. Tara gleefully clutched her hand, admiring the pretty stone.

"Jeannie! When?"

"Just last Saturday."

Considering they worked side-by-side daily at the Happy Hearts Bookshop, Tara was amazed that

Jeannie had been able to keep her engagement a secret. "And you didn't say a word?"

Jeannie blushed hotly. "I didn't want to mention it until I had the ring. Dave and I picked it out together this morning."

"How lovely!" Tara leapt from her chair and hugged Jeannie's shoulders. "I'm so happy for you. For you and Dave, both!"

But inside, Tara's heart was breaking, because she was more certain than ever that her time would never come. Besides Tara, who appeared to be the sole holdout, Jeannie was the final one of their old high school group to become engaged, and she was marrying the last eligible bachelor in Beaumont. Not that Tara was interested in Dave for herself. He and Jeannie had been an item forever, and they were an ideal match. Tara was starting to fear that the perfect match for her only existed in some fantasy realm, like those portrayed in the upbeat romance novels she loved so much.

Tara was a sucker for a happy ending. So much so, she'd lobbied the Town Council to grant her a license to open a bookstore dedicated to selling only romance novels. She owned the store and Jeannie worked as her manager. Between the two of them, they kept the ladies of Beaumont and its surrounding rural areas well supplied with happily-ever-afters in all subgenres: contemporaries, historicals...paranormals and westerns... There was something for everyone at the Happy Hearts Bookshop. And there was someone for everyone inside each tale they sold. If only Tara's truth mirrored her fiction.

****

Heath finished his after-dinner cordial at his favorite table beside the roaring fireplace. He'd enjoyed most of the Chianti with his meal and would be corking the rest and taking it home. A heavy rain was starting to fall outside, pockmarking the sidewalk beneath the streetlamp's glow. Umbrellas bloomed and couples huddled together, avoiding the sudden downpour, as thunder boomed above.

One woman partnered with a tall slender man looked familiar. She laughed and turned to face her date, latching onto the lapels of his overcoat. Then she was kissing him wildly, as he held his big golf umbrella lazily askew. Rain splatter lightly speckled the lovers but they kept on kissing, lost in each other in the storm. Heath marveled at their spectacle, knowing they were oblivious to the rest of the world.

"Young love, huh?" his waitress said, setting the to-go bag containing his corked bottle of wine on the table.

"Yeah." He smiled up at his server, extracting a few large bills from his wallet and placing them in the slim leather holder with the check.

"Need change from that?"

"No, thanks." Heath stood, his gaze once again flitting to the street-side window. The lovers had broken apart in laughter when they realized they'd both gotten sprayed. The man pulled a handkerchief from an inside pocket and gently dabbed off their clothing, before the couple walked arm in arm toward the restaurant.

Heath gaped in disbelief. He recognized them both. The man was a professional competitor, and it appeared he'd been trying to best Heath personally as well. Theirs obviously wasn't a new relationship, and the woman was...*Caroline.*

She nearly bumped into Heath, jostling in the restaurant door while trying to avoid her companion's wet umbrella as he closed it. "Heath!"

"I'm a little stunned to see you, too." He slowly perused the man, keeping his countenance steady. "Will, this is an unexpected...surprise."

Will's neck reddened at his collarbone beneath his crewneck sweater. "It's been a while, Heath." He extended a hand but Heath declined the gesture.

"I guess you weren't kidding," Heath said to Caroline.

Her face flushed but her eyes were cold. "Three years is a very long time." She shot a look at Will, who stood there stymied. He glanced from Caroline to Heath.

"You two *are* broken up?"

Caroline attempted to steer Will toward the dining room. "Of course."

"Since this morning." Heath summarily scrutinized Caroline. "That's a mighty fast recovery."

"This morning? Wait." Will waved off the maître d', and addressed his date. "You told me in September that—?"

"*September*?" Heath shook his head at Caroline. "Wow."

"What's that mean?" Will viewed Caroline suspiciously, and she began to stammer.

"I...I...just—"

Heath bowed their way. "I'll leave you both to it." Then he stepped out the door and opened his own umbrella. No rain could have felt more cleansing than the rain tonight.

There he'd been beating himself up over his poor treatment of Caroline, and *she'd* been the one catting around on him! A huge burden of guilt was lifted from Heath's shoulders, and he felt completely *free* again. Free to do what he wanted.

****

A little while later, Heath sat at his kitchen table with two Chianti bottles: the one he'd brought home from the restaurant and the one he'd found on Tybee Island. If he knew nothing else, he conceded that Irish Lass had excellent taste in wine. He'd enjoyed his Chianti tonight immensely. And, tonight wasn't done yet, he thought, helping himself to another glass.

The older Chianti bottle seemed to be calling him, prodding him to open it once again and release the magic genie in a bottle, which was actually the scrolled-up note. Now that Heath was a free man, he could write to her. Simply for the fun of it and nothing more... Heath had never been to Ireland, but he wouldn't mind visiting. *If it came to that.*

Heath took another slug of wine, noting he was letting his imagination run away with him. And that imagination painted a very different picture of a woman on a beach. She wasn't stuffy and uptight like Caroline, but rather wildly free-spirited...running and dancing through the waves. In Heath's mind's eye, he could see her, and she wasn't a blonde. She was a redhead. He squinted his eyes in thought, a different image appearing. No, not a redhead; a brunette, with rich auburn highlights in her hair.

She skipped through the shallows, her laughter tittering over the waves, and the musical sound lifted Heath's spirit high among the billowy clouds. He leaned back in his chair, savoring the fantasy of a different kind of life, with a different sort of partner. Someone who honestly adored him, and whom he cherished in return. A woman he would follow anywhere. And he was chasing her down the shore...

The sea nymph laughed again then turned to glance over her shoulder. Heath was desperate to see her face and gaze into her eyes. Were they blue like the sky or dark like the mane that flowed behind her as she leapt through the surf? Perhaps even an enchanting shade of green? But as she spun toward him, Heath's fantasy bubble popped and the entire illusion disappeared. He opened his eyes and shook his head, setting down his wine. And, in that instant, Heath knew what he had to do. It didn't matter where in the world she was, he had to write to Irish Lass, simply to verify that she really existed.

Even if the two of them weren't meant for each other, it was important for Irish Lass to know that she wasn't alone. That there were others out there who appreciated her sense of adventure. That at least one man in Savannah considered himself smart enough to handle a measured dare. Whether or not Irish Lass would consider him sexy, Heath had no idea. He supposed he could leave that up to her to decide.

Chapter Four

THE NEXT MORNING, Tara logged onto her computer at the Happy Hearts Bookshop and was greeted by the usual slew of messages. There were vendor and distributor e-mails, digests from the newsletter lists she subscribed to, and updates from her Facebook groups, including the Romantic Hearts Book Club. Tara didn't have the wherewithal to sort through them, and especially dreaded seeing what her friends at Romantic Hearts were up to. She was still digesting Jeannie's good news, and wasn't certain she could stomach anyone else's.

Apart from a serious boyfriend in college and few short-term relationships afterwards, Tara had spent most of her thirty-two years alone. Maybe Jeannie was right, and it was because Tara was being too picky. But, seriously? Was it really asking too much that a man have all his teeth? Tara thought back to the grizzled lobsterman her landlady, Ruth, had tried to set her up with, and numerous other poor matches that had come her way over the years.

Tara didn't need a guy who was drop-dead gorgeous. She'd settle for reasonably well groomed. An education wouldn't hurt either. Not to mention a solid career. She also wanted someone she could actually converse with. Maybe even somebody with a sense of humor, and a spark of adventure, too. A man willing to take risks—but calculated ones. Oh! And also have fun! An old fuddy-duddy certainly wasn't for her. Tara sighed heavily, thinking that maybe Jeannie had nailed it. Perhaps she *was* being too picky.

Boyfriends weren't like something you could order from a catalogue. You couldn't simply select the model and the color of their eyes...and hair. Or even their height for that matter. Though Tara would prefer someone just around six feet tall. *Oh, what's the use?* She repeatedly clicked her mouse, deleting the typical morning barrage of spam mail. Then she got to a message from H.Wellington@... and her heart stilled. Its subject line read: Your Message in a Bottle.

Tara clicked open the e-mail, her pulse pounding. To her disappointment, there wasn't much there. Just a very direct query.

Were you rescued?

There wasn't anything else, not even a signature line. Tara's breath quickened. Perhaps the person who'd discovered her bottle was feeling her out, by trying to see if she was still available. But honestly, why would she tell *him*? She didn't even know who H.Wellington was! The fact that he hadn't identified himself more fully set her weirdly on edge. Perhaps there was something untoward about him? Maybe he had homicidal tendencies and was running from the law?

No, that didn't make sense. A true murderer wouldn't care if she'd already found someone. He'd try to begin a correspondence anyway, and attempt to lure her in. And, he probably wouldn't use his real name. H.Wellington sounded pretty legitimate. Plus, a little high-end, to tell the truth... *H* could be a staid older gentleman in his sixties, the sort who golfed more than worked anymore. Tara was starting to question her own motives in sending that message in a bottle. She'd meant every word at the time. But she'd never really expected to receive a response.

Tara thumped her fingers against the store countertop that housed her computer then fired off her rapidly typed reply. If she never heard back from him, at least she'd learned that her bottle had landed *somewhere*. And, if she *did*, that might mark H.Wellington as a serious contender.

Assuming he was under retirement age, and still had all his choppers.

****

Heath exited the board meeting in the large conference room with floor-to-ceiling glass windows. Though he'd done so previously at the table, he thanked each of his directors once again for presenting their ideas, supplying cordial parting handshakes to them all. Heath had a great team in place and appreciated their help in keeping this giant ship running.

He passed his administrative assistant on his way back to his office and the young woman in her early twenties looked up with a smile. The slight brunette with tortoiseshell glasses wore her hair in a tight bun and was always impeccably dressed. She was also newly engaged, making her smile sparkle just as a much as the gleaming gemstone on her hand. "Can I get you a coffee, boss?"

"Coffee would be great, Kristin. Thanks."

She must have anticipated Heath's response, because Kristin had his java ready in record time. She carried it toward his desk and set it down carefully in the paper cup from the private coffee shop on the corner. "I know you didn't work magic by making this coffee suddenly appear," Heath said with a grateful chuckle.

"Magic, no." Kristin shared a wry smile. "But I did dash down to get it the moment the boardroom doors opened."

"Good call." Heath took a grateful sip of the double-shot latte. His favorite. "Thank you."

"Will there be anything else?"

"If you could bring me this morning's financial reports, that would be great. The Chancellor file, too, if you don't mind," Heath added, referring to the folder containing information on the various entities Wellington International planned to acquire by the end of the year.

"Of course." Kristin departed at a smart clip, accentuating her efficiency. Kristin didn't waste anything, most especially his time, and Heath valued her efforts. He intended to make that clear by giving her a very generous Christmas bonus.

Once his assistant had gone, Heath took a seat at his desk and turned his attention on his computer screen. Several e-mails waited in his in-box. He opened the second-to-last one first. It was the one he'd been secretly hoping for all day.

But, instead of answering his inquiry, that sassy Irish Lass had turned things right back around.

Who wants to know?

Heath's brow shot skyward as he set his fingers on the keyboard. By the virtue of her reply, she'd basically answered his question. Irish Lass likely wouldn't have answered if she was already involved with someone, certainly not if she considered the relationship serious.

He was tempted to answer right away, but decided to wait and finish his coffee. After he did, he carefully crafted his response.

I'm a banker in Savannah.

Heath scratched that.

My name is—

No good, either. Heath pondered the blank screen, feeling as if anything he could say would sound inadequate. Or worse, staged.... He wasn't even sure why he was writing back, beyond the fact that he felt compelled to. Irish Lass had now issued Heath not one challenge—but two. And, he d always had difficulty backing down on a dare.

On one hand, he couldn't help but find her new question somewhat ballsy. After all, she was the one who'd tossed out the bottle. Didn't Heath have the right to know more about her? At the same time, he couldn't exactly blame a woman for being cautious. There were a lot of weirdos out there, and Irish Lass had no way to discern whether or not Heath was among them.

He reasoned it probably wouldn't hurt to tell her a little more about himself. Besides, she was all the way across the Atlantic Ocean in Ireland. It wasn't exactly like she lived in a neighboring state and could easily track him down. He tried again.

Hello, Irish Lass. Here's a little more about me—

A little more? How would he pick and choose? What precisely should he say? Then, a brilliant thought occurred. Heath didn't have to say anything at all! He could solve his problem with just one click.

Chapter Five

TARA STARED AT the e-mail agog. "I can't believe this," she said in a breathy whisper. "The guy just sent his resume!"

Jeannie stood by the book display near the front window where she was taking inventory. "Which guy?"

"I, uh...er..." Tara's face steamed as she addressed her friend. "...heard from the man who found my bottle."

Jeannie's expression brightened. "*And*?"

Tara quickly scanned through the lengthy attachment. "He runs some sort of bank in Savannah."

"Georgia? That's fun!" Jeannie's gaze darted to the window where light flecks of snow fell outside. "And a heck of a lot warmer than here."

Tara was still musing over the odd attachment. "What did he think he was doing? Applying for a job?"

"I don't know. Maybe." Jeannie shrugged and shuffled a pile of books to one side after counting them.

"I think it's pretty exciting, actually." She gave an impish giggle. "That you heard from someone." She paused to study Tara. "How old is he?"

"Can't tell for sure, but from his college graduation date, I'd guess four years older than me." Tara held up one hand and kept reading. "But he's got a business degree, too, from Wharton. He went to the University of Virginia undergrad."

"Brainy, huh?" Jeannie was clearly impressed.

"He appears to have done well for himself," Tara said. "Worked in wealth management before assuming the family business, it seems."

"Wealth management," Jeannie said dreamily. "I like the sound of that!" She met Tara's eyes. "Do you suppose he's rich?"

"I doubt very seriously that he's struggling to make rent," Tara answered, recalling that she needed to pay her landlady. Due to slow sales in September, her rent was two weeks past due, but her landlady had a big heart, so she tended to cut Tara slack. She also had a soft spot for entrepreneurs. Ruth Evans had started her own business, the Beaumont Bakery, thirty-three years ago. She'd only sold it recently to a younger couple about Tara's age in order to retire. Tara rented an upstairs apartment that sat over Mrs. Evans's old barn, at the back of her fifty-acre property and abutting the water.

Tara's apartment was small but cozy, with its own woodstove and a spectacular view of Beaumont Bay and its amazingly dramatic tides. When the tide came in, the cove beyond Mrs. Evans's backyard gleamed with glistening blue waters. But—when the tide went out—there was nothing to be seen for miles and miles but expansive mudflats stretching beneath the craggy boulders lining the shore.

"You're probably right about that," Jeannie answered. "I'll bet the guy doesn't even *pay* rent. From what you say, I'm sure he owns his home."

"Yeah," Tara said wistfully, before glancing back through the resume. There was contact information provided, as well as a list of references. This was apparently a professional curriculum vitae that Heath used in his business dealings. From the information given, Tara surmised his bank was involved in a lot of mergers and acquisitions.

"Well, banking's good, right?" Jeannie commented. "You like bankers!"

"My dad is a teller, Jeannie," Tara stoically reminded her friend.

"Yeah? So? Maybe he and Mr. Resume would have something in common."

Tara wasn't so sure about that. While her dad had worked hard his entire life, he only had a high school education and didn't think much of big businessmen. Mostly, he was skeptical of them, arguing that too many of them wanted to take over the world.

That's the kind of talk her dad picked up at the docks while hanging around his fisherman friends, many of whom had seen their livelihoods compromised by enormous discount warehouses that sold flash-frozen fish products in bulk, and at rock-bottom prices.

"What's his name, anyway?" Jeannie prodded. She finished scribbling some notes on her clipboard then walked over to the stool where Tara sat facing her computer. Tara swiveled around to face her.

"Heath...Wellington."

"You going to look him up? Do an Internet search? I'll bet you're dying to know what he looks like!"

Tara was already one step ahead of her. She searched his name and location, and...*bingo*! There he was, a dreamy corporate guy with wavy brown hair and dark brown eyes. He apparently attended a lot of society events, and in nearly every photo he had a beautiful blonde on his arm. The same blonde.

Jeannie hovered over her shoulder. "Wow, hubba-hubba! Nice-looking guy! What about the woman? Girlfriend?"

"Maybe a former one?" Tara asked hopefully. She'd hate to think of Heath as the cheating kind. Particularly as she was just starting to form her opinion of him.

"Yeah, you're probably right. I mean, why else would he write to you?"

"Don't worry. I intend to ask him."

"Yeah?"

"Yeah. But I'm going to do something else first."

"What's that?"

Tara adjusted the collar of the silk blouse she wore beneath her charcoal gray pullover. When she peered back at Jeannie, she grinned. "Send him *my* resume."

****

"Touché!" Heath opened Irish Lass's e-mail and smiled. She hadn't written one word. She had merely sent an attachment, just as he'd done. Heath scanned through Tara's credentials with interest. She'd gone to Tulane on an academic scholarship, and had worked at an independent bookstore part-time while in school. After holding a few local management jobs in the interim, she'd returned to her hometown in Maine to open a bookshop of her own. Tara had double-majored in English and economics, an unusual combination that appeared to have served her well.

Heath couldn't help but be impressed by what she'd accomplished while still in her twenties. He was also oddly relieved to learn she didn't live in Ireland after all. With a name like Tara McAdams, she was clearly of Irish extraction. Though, from everything on her resume, it appeared that she'd grown up in Maine. So the "Irish Lass" moniker must have referred to her heritage rather than her nationality.

He took a moment to find a map of Beaumont, Maine online, deciding Tara might as well be across the Atlantic. The driving distance between Savannah and Beaumont was nearly twenty hours. Heath could hop a plane from Atlanta to Dublin in half the time!

The funny thing was, Dublin didn't intrigue him at the moment. Yet, something about Beaumont was beginning to seem awfully interesting. Tomorrow, he'd write to Tara again and share something a little more personal about himself.

If past was prologue. she might even follow suit.

Chapter Six

"So," BYRON ASKED, when they met for their regular Wednesday afternoon golf date. "How did things go with Caroline while I was on my honeymoon?"

Heath picked out his driver and teed off, swinging hard. The ball crowned in a perfect arc then landed on the green, bouncing twice before rolling toward the first hole.

"Nice shot!"

"They didn't," Heath said, answering Byron's earlier question.

Byron started to tee off next, then halted mid-swing.

"Wait a minute..." He planted his driver on the ground, leaning into it. "What do you mean, *they didn't*?"

"I mean *they didn't*." Heath motioned for Byron to take his shot, and Byron did, his ball landing a foot behind Heath's.

"You didn't ask her, you mean?" Byron asked, as Heath selected a putter.

"Nope."

"No way, buddy." Byron shoved his hands in his pockets and held his ground. "You're not getting off the hook that easily."

Heath met Byron's confounded gaze. Byron had light brown eyes and shortly cropped golden brown hair. "Let's just say the timing wasn't right," he answered, attempting to move past him.

Byron's brow rose quizzically. "Then, what gives? I thought you had a proposal on the table?"

"*Had* is the operative word." Heath soundly patted Byron's arm. "Thank goodness I never followed through with it."

"Because?"

Heath lined up his next shot with laser-like focus.

"Caroline was running around on me."

Byron's retort rang with disbelief. "*Noooo*. She didn't?"

"Oh yeah, she did. And with Will Barrymore, no less. She was apparently stringing us both along to see who would propose first." Heath tapped his ball and easily sank it.

"That skank!"

"Yeah, well." Heath shrugged mildly, retrieving his ball. "Let bygones be bygones. That's what I say."

"You're taking this awfully well. If I didn't know better..." Byron viewed him suspiciously, as he withdrew his own putter from his bag. "I'd say you already had someone else, too."

"Let's just say I found a genie in a bottle."

"What's that supposed to mean?" Byron asked, stepping past him.

"I found an empty Chianti bottle floating out on Tybee Beach."

Byron glanced over his shoulder. "And?"

"A note was in it."

"From a damsel in distress?" Byron asked, teasing.

"Pretty much, yeah."

Byron's eyes widened in disbelief. "You're kidding, right?"

"A very capable damsel, though."

"Oh, *really*?"

"She's smart. Talented. Has gumption. Started her own business in her twenties."

"You found all that on a note in a bottle?"

Heath laughed good-naturedly. "Nope. Not there."

"Wait a minute... But how did you—?" Byron's eyes lit in understanding. "You contacted her, didn't you?"

"Yep."

Byron shot him an exasperated look. He clearly felt like he was pulling teeth, trying to extract some information about this mystery woman. "*And*?"

"And, nothing. She sent me her resume."

"*Interesting.*"

"Yeah, she is. Very "

"Pretty?" Byron asked in a leading tone.

"What's that they say?" Heath slowly shook his head. "Beauty's in the eye of the beholder?"

"That bad, huh? A real barker."

"Byron!"

"Well, sorry," he said, looking like he wasn't. "I'm just saying, when a man dodges that sort of question—"

"That's because I haven't seen her."

"Come on. She must have left cyber footprints somewhere."

"True. She belongs to a group called the Romantic Hearts Book Club."

"Whoa, sounds a little scary."

"Says the newlywed," Heath bantered.

"There were no photos of her there?"

"All I got was an icon. Of a coffee mug and a book with a rose on it."

"Could be setting yourself up for something dangerous."

"Who says I'm setting myself up for anything?"

Byron met his gaze dead-on. "Educated guess."

****

"What am I supposed to do with this?" Tara shouted, looking up from the e-mail.

"With what?" Jeannie asked, as she carted a full box of new books across the room.

"Heath sent me his Top Ten lists!"

"Top Tens?" Jeannie asked, confounded.

"Top ten songs, top ten movies, top ten books, and top ten favorite foods!"

"Wow."

"I know. A lot more personal than a resume, right?" But in another way, it really wasn't. Heath could just as easily have formulated these answers for a guest spot on a blog, assuming bankers even did that sort of thing.

Scanning through them, Tara was astounded to see they had many favorites in common. In the food and music departments, anyway... Heath's book and film choices tended to veer more toward action-adventure and hard-boiled mysteries. "You're never going to guess his favorite flavor of ice cream."

Jeannie set down her box and grinned. "It isn't?"

Tara raised her eyebrows and replied in near disbelief, "Pistachio."

****

Later that evening, Heath carried a nice big bowl of his favorite ice cream and a bourbon into his living room and sat down in a wing chair by the roaring fire. While it was still warm during the day, the nights were growing chilly and Heath savored the chance to use his wood-burning fireplace whenever possible.

He set his laptop on his knees and flipped it open. The first e-mail that caught his eye came from Tara McAdams. When he scanned through her Top Ten lists, his spoon slipped from his fingers, clanking loudly against the side of the bowl.

No way—but it was. She was either putting him on, or... He glanced down at his green dessert then back up at his computer screen. Tara's favorite ice cream was also pistachio.

Heath had the sudden urge to call her and hear her voice. Would she speak in cool crisp tones like a northerner or draw out her words like the women down south due to her time spent in New Orleans? Heath couldn't wait to find out.

He snagged his phone off the end table beside him, and pulled up Tara's resume on his computer. Her contact information was right there. All he had to do was dial.

****

Tara sat on her futon, wrapped in a throw blanket and reading by her woodstove. Her cell phone rang, but she almost ignored the call—thinking the unrecognized number might belong to a solicitor. Then, at the last minute, curiosity got the better of her and she decided to answer.

"Is it really pistachio?" a man asked without preamble. His voice was as smooth as silk and smoky like well-aged scotch. There was a mild lilt at the end of his syllables. A southern accent, but very subtle. Sophisticated and controlled. "I would have pegged you for mocha chocolate chip?" Tara's face heated when she realized he must be Heath.

"And I would have pegged you for *Georgia peach*," she answered with an intentionally sassy twang. Tara gathered her resolve, attempting to sound pleasant and only mildly flirty. "I don't have to guess how you got my number; I suppose I already know," she said, referring to the fact that it had appeared on her resume.

"Since you didn't call, I decided I had to."

"To ask about ice cream?" she teased.

"No..." He drew out the word to let the weight of it sink in. "I was angling for an introduction."

Tara's heart fluttered and her head felt light. "Heath Wellington," she said fake primly, though her pulse was racing. "I'm Tara McAdams. It's nice to meet you." Then she giggled before adding jokingly, "*There*, how was that?"

His laughter rumbled. "I'd say pretty perfect."

"You sound different from how I imagined."

"Oh?"

"Younger, I guess." *And a heck of a lot sexier*, she thought, but didn't say.

Heath chuckled again and she could almost imagine a sparkle in his dark brown eyes. "Let's hope that's a plus."

"I didn't know at first…" Tara hesitated a beat before continuing. "I mean, before seeing your resume, I wasn't sure you were even close to my age."

"You took a pretty big gamble with that bottle," he teased. "Anyone could have found it. Even an octogenarian, it's true."

"Maybe an octogenarian wouldn't have been able to use the Internet?"

"You don't know my Granddad," Heath said warmly.

"Does he live in Savannah?"

"Yeah."

"Other family, too?"

"Just him for now. My parents and brother live in Charlotte," he answered. "How about you? Got family nearby? Up there in faraway Beaumont, Maine?"

"It's not so faraway to me," she answered sunnily. "And yeah, I've got my dad here." After a pause, she decided to brave it. "Heath?"

"Yes?"

"Can I ask you a question?"

"Take a stab at two, if you'd like."

"The blonde...? The one who was with you in the photos..."

"The lady's been sleuthing," he hummed into the receiver and Tara's cheeks burned hot.

"Is she...? What I mean is, you looked pretty close."

"We were, for all of three years."

"Three years. Wow. That's a long time."

"I know."

"But, it's over?"

"Yes."

"What ended it?" Tara asked, realizing she didn't necessarily have a right to know. Still, she couldn't help from asking, just in case he'd volunteer. When there was silence down the line, she rushed in with an apology, understanding she'd overstepped her bounds. "I'm sorry, I—"

"Let's just say a twist of fate," Heath answered evenly.

"Fate?"

"You do believe in it?" he challenged mildly. "You run a bookstore dedicated to romance, after all.

And, you're a member of the Romantic Hearts Book Club."

"Aha!" she cut in with a playful edge. "So I'm not the only one who's been *sleuthing*. Hmm."

"Guilty as charged." Tara heard a glass tinkle in the background and guessed he was drinking something. Bourbon on the rocks or maybe a brandy? "You're a hard woman to pin down online."

"Maybe that's because I like my privacy."

"Privacy, huh." He sighed heavily, sounding almost wistful. "What a concept."

"I suppose you don't get much of that?"

"In some ways, Savannah is a small town."

"Do you travel a lot?"

"Sometimes more than I'd like. More often than not, it's to New York."

"I like the city."

"Yeah, me too. Except for when I'm there on business," he added with a chuckle. "Which is always."

"Maybe you should try going for fun sometime?"

"Yeah, well." The cadence of his voice picked up as he answered. "Maybe I will."

"I'm really glad you called," she told him. "You're very easy to talk to."

"So are you.'

"Will you call again?"

"Nope." Tara's heart sank, before he added quickly, "I want you to call me."

"When?"

"Anytime. Surprise me."

****

Tara hit End Call, her fingers trembling. She couldn't believe it, but it was true! She'd just spoken to the man who'd found her message in a bottle. Heath definitely had a daring side. He'd called her, hadn't he? And he most definitely was smart. And, boy oh boy, did he ever sound sexy.

Tara sighed and threw her head back with a giggle, as she clutched her cell phone to her chest. He'd called! Heath had actually called! And he seemed absolutely terrific! She couldn't wait to talk to him again. Now, all Tara had to do was decide when.

Chapter Seven

JEANNIE GRABBED TARA'S hand and squealed when Tara told her the news. They were seated at a small table at the little sandwich shop by the docks. It was their custom to close the bookstore at lunchtime once a week to do a girls' lunch and take a breather. They'd both ordered fried fish sandwiches and hot coffee, and sat by a window overlooking the bay and the scattered lobster pot buoys that bobbed beyond it.

The tide was high and the fishing boats that were typically moored near the mouth of the cove were out to sea. Brisk winds blew, kicking up white-tipped waves, as gulls soared beneath a clear blue sky.

"That's so great, Tara," Jeannie said excitedly. "I can't believe Heath called! How did he sound?"

"Gorgeous!" Tara ducked her head and giggled. "I mean, seriously, he did."

"Yeah well, you're pretty gorgeous, too," Jeannie said, surveying her. "What with those ebony locks and those dark green eyes... Not to mention your girlish figure!"

"Shut up," Tara said, but she was smiling.

A realization hit Jeannie and she gasped. "Heath doesn't even know what you look like, does he?"

Tara shrugged. "No, and it doesn't seem to matter."

"Go on!"

"I mean, he hasn't asked for a picture or anything."

"Are you going to send one?"

"I don't know." Tara lowered her voice and raised an eyebrow. "I kind of like being a woman of mystery."

Jeannie rollicked with laughter. "Sure. Okay. Anything you say! Whatever you're doing seems to be working for you." She took a bite of her sandwich then set it down. "Have you thought about what you're going to say when you call him?"

"Honestly?" Tara rolled her eyes. "I have no idea!"

"You could always ask him to come visit."

"Stop."

"I mean it. Maybe he'd like Maine?"

"Yeah, so? Maybe I'd like Savannah, but I'm not going there, either."

"Why not?"

"That might put me at a disadvantage, being on his turf."

"You think he'd feel disadvantaged here?"

"No," Tara answered truthfully. "Heath sounds like a man who can pretty much take care of himself— anywhere on the globe."

Jeannie widened her eyes and leaned forward. "This is so crazy! Imagine, Tara! Heath Wellington might just be the man of your dreams!"

"I wouldn't go putting the cart before the horse just yet," Tara answered reasonably. But beneath her calm exterior, Tara's pulse was racing. It seemed silly. *Impossible*. But way down deep in her heart Tara held a tiny glimmer of hope.

With her and Heath both running their own businesses and them living several states apart, the odds were certainly against anything serious developing between them. Then again, sometimes physical limitations didn't matter. Wasn't that what the sign above the door in her bookshop read? *Love knows no bounds.*

"All right, I'll stop jumping the gun," Jeannie agreed, "but only if you promise me one thing."

"What's that?"

"That you'll name your first-born child after me."

Tara playfully slapped her arm. "*Jean-nie!*"

"I know, I know," she said giddily. "I just can't help hoping for you."

Truth be told, Tara couldn't help hoping for herself, either. "Yeah," she said with a warm blush. "Thanks."

****

Two weeks later, Tara phoned Heath on Saturday morning. Since she'd first returned his phone call a few days after receiving his, they'd e-mailed, texted, and talked nearly every day, with each of them taking turns initiating the phone calls. They spoke about nothing in particular and things that came to mind.

Very easily, they'd slipped into the routine of sharing tidbits about their days: Tara's funny customer stories and Heath's reports on humorous office antics. Like the time one of the office assistants left her celebrity crush's photo on the copier, then claimed she was merely making a collage of successful financial figures.

Tara had the middle-aged lady who came in every Wednesday, at exactly eleven o'clock, to ask about the new books that had arrived that week. She'd studiously browse through them then leave without purchasing even one. Tara and Jeannie suspected that was because she was hunting down her top picks at the neighborhood library. But that was okay with them. The woman was very friendly and liked to talk books, so they enjoyed seeing her on a regular basis.

Tara carried her mug of coffee to the tiny table nestled in a nook by the window overlooking the bay. A blanket of white covered the ground and minute snowflakes twirled through the air. But a little wintry weather wouldn't prevent the people of Beaumont from conducting business as usual. All of them were used to it.

She had about an hour before her shop opened so she decided to dedicate part of it to speaking with Heath. Their conversations always lightened her heart and lifted her spirits. Already, she'd grown accustomed to them and looked forward to hearing his voice. She caught him in a jovial mood and sounding wide-awake.

"Good morning," he said pleasantly, instantly recognizing her voice.

"I hope I'm not calling too early?"

"Been awake for hours," he said. "Just sitting here reading the paper and drinking my coffee."

"I'm having my coffee, too."

"Costa Rican dark blend?"

"You know me so well," she said, laughing.

"I'm starting to know you better, that's true."

"How's the weather in Savannah?" she asked lightly.

"Getting colder. And, there?"

"We got a foot of snow last night."

Heath chuckled loudly. "It's not even November."

"No, but it will be soon."

"Yes, I've been thinking a lot about that."

"Me, too," Tara offered. "Our shipment of holiday books came in this week."

"Romantic holiday reads?" he teased.

Tara grinned. "Absolutely!"

"Tara?"

"Huh?"

"Can I ask you something about your message in a bottle?" There was a serious note in his voice, and

Tara reflected on the fact that he hadn't broached this topic to date. Perhaps he thought it was finally time. He was likely curious.

"Sure."

"Why did you send it?"

"Well, I..." Tara swallowed hard. "I don't know. It was a lark, I guess. Me and my friends were on this island—"

"Enchanted Island?"

"How did you know?"

"The hotel stationery was a dead giveaway."

Tara laughed in understanding. "Yes, that one. A group of us from my online book club got together there, and on our final night we all kind of did the bottle toss as a dare."

"You mean there are other bottles floating around out there?"

"I assume so. That is, apart from Meg's. Someone already found hers. It actually washed back up on Enchanted Island."

"What happened there?"

Tara felt herself blush. "She's getting married."

"I see," he said after a pause. "How many of you did this?"

"Twelve altogether."

"Imagine that." Heath sounded intrigued. "I might have found somebody else's message."

"One of my friends'? Of course that's possible."

"But I'm glad that I didn't," he went on. "I'm pleased that I found yours." His voice deepened. "Because I like you, Tara. I like you a lot."

"You barely know me," she said, caught off guard.

"Hardly matters, does it?"

"Why not?"

"Because you like me, too."

Tara's skin burned hot. "It's true, I find you...interesting."

"Interesting? Um-hum. I'll take that over boring, any day." He waited a moment before asking, "Tara...?" From the sound of his voice, he was leading up to something.

"Yes?" she asked nervously.

"About what you wrote specifically... Was that just a ploy to get a response? Or, did you really mean it?"

"I...er...well..." Tara took a sip of coffee, biding her time.

"It's okay, either way," he said, letting her off the hook. "It's not like I'm feeling pressure. Frankly, I thought the idea was cute."

"Cute?" Tara asked weakly.

"It was very innovative, that note you wrote. That's why I felt compelled to answer. You made me want to know more about you."

Tara felt fire creep into her cheeks. "I'm really glad that you did... Answer, I mean." She measured her words, feeling awkward about what she was going to say next. "Heath, I think I should make it clear... What I'm saying is, I'm really happy that you got in touch, but I don't want you to think... Or feel like you have to—"

"I rarely do anything I don't want, Tara. If you don't know that about me already, you'll learn that soon enough." After a beat, he added, "You know, all this phone chatting is great, but I thought it might be nice if we could see each other sometime." Tara's heart thumped wildly. "In person."

"Well, I..." Tara hesitated, her head reeling. What was he suggesting? That he might come to Maine, or that she should visit Savannah?

"I was wondering if I could take you out for coffee..." He paused for effect. "In New York?"

Tara caught her breath. "New York?"

"A wise woman I know once suggested I give the city a try—just for fun."

"Yes, but—"

"I understand it's a distance for you."

"It is for you, as well."

"That's why I thought we'd meet in the middle?"

Tara anxiously twisted a lock of her hair around her finger. The idea seemed so exciting, but also a little dangerous. Although they'd been conversing long-distance, she still didn't know many things about him, besides what she'd found on his resume and had read online. "We'll meet in a public place?" she asked a tad unsurely.

Heath laughed warmly, putting her at ease. "No problem. How about in the bar of our hotel?"

"Hotel? Oh, no. No, no, no... I'm really sorry, Heath. I'm afraid you've got it wrong. I'm not—"

"*That sort of girl.* I know. That's why I've booked us separate rooms." He named a ritzy hotel on Fifth Avenue, and Tara was tempted to pinch herself to be sure this was actually happening.

"Wow. *My.* I...I'm really not sure."

"I got two tickets to a show," he said, temptingly. "A great one."

"*The* show? The one everybody is talking about?"

"If coffee goes well, maybe you'll let me take you to a matinee—and then out to dinner? If it doesn't, there's no obligation. You'll be free to go, or stay and attend the theater anyway. I won't burden you with my presence." Tara somehow found it impossible to imagine Heath's presence could be a burden to anybody. Ever.

"You'd do all this just to meet me?" she asked, still mildly shocked.

"Yes."

"But why?"

He waited a while before answering. Finally, he said, "Because every morning for the past sixteen days I've woken up thinking about you. A woman I haven't even met in person. And no one has ever had that sort of impact on me."

Maybe he felt that way now, but would his perspective change after he'd met her face to face? Tara led a quiet, simple life in a place that was a far cry from the glitzy social circles of Savannah. Unlike Heath's former girlfriend, who'd appeared totally in her element, Tara wasn't practiced at attending elegant soirees, or comfortable with stuffy conversation.

She pursed her lips, considering his offer. "Can I take some time to think about it?"

"Of course."

"Great."

"Only, if you could decide by Thursday, that might help so I can book our flights."

"*Our* flights?'

"A gentleman wouldn't ask a lady out for coffee expecting her to pay."

"Yeah, but plane tickets?"

"Just say the word, and I'll have my assistant arrange it."

"I couldn't let you—"

"It would be my pleasure."

"When?" she asked in stunned disbelief.

"Next Saturday."

"One week from today?"

"I'm sorry if that's not enough lead-time. I was just able to grab these tickets—"

"No, no." Tara caught her breath, her heart pounding. "It's fine." Was Tara really considering this? Getting whisked off to the Big Apple by Heath Wellington for a latte? It sounded awfully exciting and nerve-racking and adventuresome...

Did Tara honestly have the guts to go for it? That's when she reminded herself that Heath had been brave enough to respond to her message in a bottle. She'd been impressed when he'd taken the leap to contact her. And everything she'd learned about him since had only made her like him more.

"Okay," she said, at last. "I'll do it! But just coffee in the bar, okay? No promises beyond that."

"Excellent," he replied. "Do you mind if I give my assistant your number?"

Chapter Eight

"REMIND ME AGAIN," her dad said. "Just where are you going tomorrow?" Richard McAdams was a stocky man with prematurely gray hair and dark eyes.

Tara finished chewing her bite of meatloaf, and took a sip of water. Her dad had asked her to dinner, and it was delicious as always. "I already told you, I'm going to New York to meet a friend."

"For coffee," he repeated blandly. "What's wrong with your friend? Why can't she come here?"

"She...um..." Tara prepared another forkful of mashed potatoes and gobbled it up gratefully. "...is busy."

"You're too old to talk with your mouth full," her dad admonished. "Who is this friend, anyway?"

Tara knew if she told him, he'd freak. Jeannie had freaked too, but in a much more positive way than Tara imagined her dad doing. Jeannie had actually been happy for her, and excited. So excited she'd helped Tara plan her whole wardrobe! One outfit for the flight and coffee. Another one for the theater and dinner—if she went. And a third for the following morning, in case Tara and Heath met for breakfast before Tara's noontime return flight. Jeannie would hold down the fort at the bookstore while she was gone.

"Somebody you don't know. A friend from..." Tara thought fast. "...college."

"What's her name?"

"Hea...Heather."

Her dad harrumphed. "If Heather's so special, why haven't you talked about her?"

"Because, Dad." Tara gave an exaggerated sigh. "We weren't actually *that* close. Just friends from the dorm."

"And yet you're flying all the way to—?"

"Will you look at the time?" Tara stood abruptly, eying the clock on the stove. "I'm really sorry. I told Jeannie I'd meet her at the bookstore to go over some last-minute instructions."

Her dad viewed her carefully. "If I didn't know better, I'd say my girl was hiding something."

Tara wanted to tell him. She really did. But she also didn't want to worry him unnecessarily and Richard McAdams was the fretting kind. "I'll be back the day after tomorrow," she said, kissing his cheek. "I'll tell you more about everything then." And Tara definitely intended to, particularly if things went well.

Meanwhile, she'd provided Jeannie with details concerning her complete itinerary so someone would know exactly where she was if there was a problem. Tara slipped into her coat and headed for the door. "Thanks so much for the meatloaf!" she said brightly. "It was yummy!"

****

Heath sat in the upscale bar decorated with plush carpets, big comfy chairs, and dripping chandeliers. Large palladium windows faced out on Fifth Avenue where Saturday afternoon shoppers bustled by. A bottle of still water and two tall glasses sat on the café table in front of him. He lifted the bottle and poured himself a glass, staying mindful of the movement in the room. Every time a new woman entered, his senses alerted and his temperature spiked. While he didn't know what Tara looked like, she would probably recognize him from the photos she'd seen online.

Though he'd had ample opportunity to ask for Tara's picture, Heath had decided to let life surprise him. Beautiful women were a dime a dozen in Savannah. But, if his relationship with Caroline had taught him anything, it was that looks weren't enough.

What really mattered was an authentic connection. Finding a person that you actually enjoyed being with—and could talk to. Heath felt like he'd already been developing that sort of relationship with Tara, sight unseen. He hoped things wouldn't change between them once they met face to face.

He straightened his tie, wondering if he'd overdressed for afternoon coffee. He wore a sweater over his dress shirt and chinos and loafers. If they went to the theater and dinner afterwards, he'd add the jacket that was hanging in the closet in his room. Because he'd been able to tell Tara was a bit nervous about meeting him in a hotel, he'd taken care to book their rooms on separate floors. Heath had also made sure Tara's room was extremely well appointed, with fresh flowers and a top-notch view of the city from the eighteenth floor.

She'd texted him earlier to say her flight was on time and that she'd see him shortly at the hotel, soon after checking in. Heath glanced at his watch, surmising she'd arrived by now and was likely upstairs in her room. Hopefully, admiring his bouquet and the view, and priming herself to think good thoughts about him.

Heath didn't know how he'd gone from finding Tara's bottle on the beach to a hotel in New York City, but in some ways he'd been on a trajectory he hadn't been able to stop. No, correct that. It was a trajectory he hadn't *wanted* to stop. Tara had captivated him from the start.

He didn't know what to expect next, which set him slightly off kilter. Heath was the consummate planner, who always orchestrated everything carefully. Yet, there was a measure of the situation here that was not within his control. Despite his best efforts at coordinating a dynamite first date, there were no guarantees that Tara would enjoy his company, or that there'd be any real chemistry between them.

"Heath?"

He turned in surprise at the soft feminine inquiry to find a gorgeous brunette standing beside him. She must have entered from the far side of the room by the lobby, rather than near the hostess stand by the street-side entrance.

Heath shifted and got to his feet, addressing the beautiful woman. While he'd decided that her looks didn't matter, he'd never expected to be greeted by a knockout. She wore a red sweater dress with a wide leather belt that matched her brown boots and accentuated her stunning figure. Her layered dark hair fell just past her shoulders in a tasteful, modern cut, and her creamy complexion was offset by sparkling green eyes. "Tara?" he asked, with pleased surprise.

Her heart-shaped mouth drew up in a smile. "Guilty as charged," she said, throwing one of his earliest retorts back at him.

Heath took her hand and an electric current ripped through him. "Thank you for coming."

"Thanks for inviting me," she said with a saucy edge.

He motioned for her to have a seat and she did, as Heath returned to his chair. "Everything all right with the room?" he asked her.

"Better than all right." Her pretty face grew animated. "It's gorgeous! With a view of Fifth Avenue and everything!"

"I'm glad that you like it," he said sincerely.

"And the flowers were..." She ducked her chin with a blush. "Very pretty, too. Thank you."

"You're welcome." Heath sat back in his chair, taking her in. "Tara McAdams, in person. It's hard to believe you're really here."

"I can hardly believe it myself," she admitted, as if she was letting him in on a secret. "I've never done anything this...impetuous!"

"Apart from sending a message in a bottle," Heath quipped and she laughed deeply.

"Yeah, there was *that*."

Suddenly, the ice was broken between them and Heath felt himself relax. "You look very nice," he told her. "You're an incredibly beautiful woman."

"And you look just like your pictures." Her cheeks colored sweetly. "No, better."

Heath liked the sound of that. She was apparently taken with him, and flirting. He flagged down a waiter then raised his brow. "What can I get you? Coffee? Tea?"

"Do you think they have Irish coffee?" she asked a tad impishly.

Heath hadn't quite expected this, but he was happy to get Tara anything she wanted. "You mean the sort with whipped cream and a good shot of whiskey?"

"It's really chilly outside," she said, as if that explained her desire for the drink.

"Yes, and windy, too," Heath agreed. He could think of no finer way to spend the next hour than sipping the hot frothy beverage with a kick, while in the company of a beautiful woman. "Two Irish coffees it is!"

****

Tara set down her tall glass coffee mug with a contented sigh. "That was *soooo* good. I've got to tell you, I haven't had a coffee like that in a long time. Not since New Orleans."

"Is Irish coffee really that hard to come by in Beaumont?"

"Oh yeah," she said with a giggle. "Pretty much everything's hard to come by in Beaumont, except lobster."

Heath laughed at this. "I like lobster."

Tara took a moment to study his sturdy build and warm brown eyes. She'd meant it when she'd said he was better looking in person than in his pictures. And in his photos, he'd looked pretty great...so that said a lot. "Me, too. But, I appreciate having variety once in a while."

"You should try low-country shrimp and grits," he suggested.

"I have, and they're delicious."

"That's right I keep forgetting you've got experience as a southern girl."

"Perhaps, but I'm not a world traveler like you."

"Traveling the world has its ups and downs."

"Oh?" It was hard for Tara to imagine that.

"The long flights can be tiring. And truthfully, when I'm traveling on business, my schedule is so packed there's not much time for sightseeing."

"That's really too bad. Have you ever thought of extending a trip?"

"I prefer to separate business and pleasure." He viewed her with interest. "Have you traveled much?"

"Not nearly as much as I'd like," she admitted honestly. "Just a little bit in the U.S. and to Enchanted Island, but I'd love to travel more overseas. Particularly to Ireland."

His dark eyes danced. "That would be fitting for an Irish Lass."

Tara's face warmed. "Yes."

Heath checked the clock above the bar against his watch. "It's almost time for the matinee. If we're going to get our seats, we should probably... What I mean is..." He appeared the tiniest bit abashed and Tara's heart melted. "If you're still interested in us going together?"

"Heath Wellington," she said surely, "I'd be delighted to go to the theater with you."

"And dinner afterwards?" he asked hopefully.

Tara grinned, marveling to herself that she was having a wonderful time. Heath was just as easy to talk to in person as he was on the phone. Plus, his countenance was truly a feast for the eyes. "Dinner afterwards sounds fine."

"Great, because I know an out-of-the-way Italian place you might like."

"Italian?"

"They make a superb pumpkin gnocchi," he said, referring to one of her favorite foods on her earlier Top Ten list. "Plus they serve a very fine Chianti." Heath winked and Tara tingled all over. She felt like a fairy princess, and she was definitely getting the royal treatment. "That sounds fabulous, Heath."

Chapter Nine

TARA AND HEATH lingered over a second bottle of Chianti at the quaint Italian restaurant. Candles flickered on red-checkered tablecloths, and patrons packed the closely-spaced tables at the cute bistro located not a mile from Times Square. The entrance was on a quiet side street, which was one reason why Bella Fortuna was favored by locals. The other had to do with the stellar quality of its food and the relatively reasonable prices, particularly given the fact that this was New York.

Heath offered to refill Tara's wine, but she declined, saying at this point she might be better off with a cappuccino. He laughed deeply at this and his laughter warmed her soul. "I hear what you're saying," he answered, setting down the bottle. "I'd probably better lay off, too. I'm sure we can cork and carry, if you'd like?"

"For later?" Tara asked lightly. She wasn't even sure what she imagined. That they'd share a few glasses in their hotel bar, or maybe on the scenic rooftop that was set up with outdoor space heaters and comfy furnishings? She'd seen it on the hotel website once Heath's assistant had booked her accommodations, and she'd thought the view incredibly romantic. Though it was bound to be chilly this time of year.

"The hotel has a rooftop terrace," Heath began and Tara blushed hotly.

"I was just thinking about that," she admitted over the rim of her wineglass.

"Were you really?" he asked, looking pleased.

The server arrived to clear their plates and Heath ordered them two cappuccinos, inquiring first whether Tara would like dessert. She would have loved some of the delicious-looking cannoli she'd seen carried by, if only she'd had the room.

Once they were alone again, Heath met her eyes. "I can't believe this is our first date," he said. "It really seems as if we've known each other longer."

Tara shrugged shyly. "I guess, in a way, we have. We've communicated a lot, anyhow."

"Yeah." His gazed roamed over her. "You know the funny thing about that? I normally don't e-mail much, or talk on the phone."

"You're one of those to-the-point businessmen," she observed.

His expression said she'd assessed him accurately. "Generally, yes."

"What's different this time?" Tara asked tentatively, hoping she knew.

He gently took her hand. "I got a message in a bottle."

Heath's touch was firm yet reassuring, like he was there to support her and not rush her in any way. Though Tara's wayward heart was racing headlong into the future. She'd never known a man like Heath. Someone so successful, and handsome and attentive... He'd completely swept her off her feet.

"You're treating me very regally," she asserted.

"I wanted to make this a memorable first date." Heath lifted her hand and kissed the back of it. Tingles skittered up Tara's arm and warmth pooled in her belly. He cocked one eyebrow and asked sexily, "How am I doing?"

Tara caught her breath. "*Very* well."

His grin said that was the answer he'd hoped for.

"Tara?"

"Yes?" she asked, her heart pounding.

"That other guy? The one who broke your heart?"

A knife twisted in her gut, when she realized he was referring to her SOS.

Heath squeezed her hand. "He was an idiot. I hope you believe that."

"Thank you," she said softly. "Thank you for saying so."

Compassion lined his face, and another emotion, as well. Tara thought she recognized it as empathy. "I know what it feels like to be let down," he said sincerely.

"I'm sorry that you've been through it, too."

"What doesn't kill us makes us stronger." He shot her a crooked smile and Tara's pulse quickened. "Wouldn't you agree?"

"Yes."

Their waiter appeared with two steaming cappuccinos and Heath released her hand, making space on the table between them. As soon as their server had gone, Heath lifted his coffee cup toward hers in a toasting motion. "Here's to our Herculean health!"

Tara chuckled merrily. "Yes," she said, clinking his cup. "Here's to us!"

Chapter Ten

THE VIEW FROM the hotel rooftop was every bit as amazing as Heath had hoped it would be. He and Tara sat on a cozy cushioned sofa by a flaming stone-crafted fire pit. Tall space heaters were positioned around the various seating groups for additional warmth, and other couples chatted happily over glasses of wine, some exchanging lighthearted stories with groups of friends. City lights sparkled against the backdrop of the inky sky, twinkling from skyscraper windows and the nearby Empire State Building, which towered just a few blocks away.

"It's really stunning," Tara said, and Heath had to agree. "Have you stayed in this hotel before?"

"Yes, but previously on business." Heath took a studied sip of wine. "I like visiting this way much better."

Tara laughed, warmly snuggled in her button-up wool coat. It had a tweed pattern—brown interlaced with gold and green—that picked up the color of her eyes. They sparkled in the firelight, and Heath thought to himself that he'd never seen a more beautiful woman. And it wasn't simply Tara's looks; it had to do with the confident way she held herself and her slightly sassy demeanor. "There's nothing wrong with taking a vacation once in a while," she said.

"When was your last one?"

She looked pensive, but only for a moment. "Last summer, at Enchanted Island."

"And, before that?"

This time, she took longer to answer. "Might have been... No, wait." Her brow knitted. "I'm afraid you've got me on that," she finally said, meeting his eyes. "The sad truth is I don't take many vacations. How about you?"

"I went to Mexico with..." he started before quickly stopping himself. Heath had no business bringing up Caroline. Truth was, he didn't really want to think about her. Especially not when he was in the company of such a spectacular woman. "Doesn't really matter who I was with." Heath set down his wine. "Anyway, a lot of the details are fuzzy."

Tara eyed him astutely. "It was her, wasn't it? The one who broke your heart?"

"She was my girlfriend, yeah. But I wouldn't give her that much credit."

"No?"

"In many ways, Caroline did me a favor. Her misdeeds cemented my decision to contact you."

"I'm starting to like this Caroline." She shot him a minxy smile and Heath's heart stuttered.

"Maybe we should drink to her?" he ventured, raising his glass.

Tara clinked her wineglass to his. "Here's to Caroline."

"Here's to moving on," he answered, taking a slug of his Chianti.

"Well, I certainly won't be toasting my ex," she answered after a beat.

"Your breakup was pretty awful, huh?" he asked sympathetically.

"We were supposed to be married." She viewed him sadly, and Heath could tell that the memories were hard on her, even now. "But, oh well..."

"What happened? I mean, you don't have to tell—"

"He proposed, then voila! Rode off into the sunset."

"I don't understand."

"Trust me on this, it was pretty hard for me to get, too." Her shoulders sagged beneath the weight of the memory. "Ned proposed right after college graduation. We'd been going out at that point for more than two years. He said..." She appeared to gather her nerve, then she continued. "He said he wanted to buy me a ring, and do the whole thing right. He made a reservation at a top-notch New Orleans restaurant. I was to meet him there at eight o'clock. There were butterflies in my stomach and everything." She sighed regretfully. "I guess I was young then, and naïve."

"Doesn't sound like you were being naïve to me," Heath responded kindly. "Merely hopeful. And, from what you said, your boyfriend had given you every reason to hope."

"Yes, he had. Right down to asking for my ring size."

"He did that outright?" Heath asked, surprised.

"A girlfriend and I went to a jewelers and they sized me. A perfect six."

"And?" Heath pressed, drawn into her heartbreaking story.

Tara gazed at him sadly. "He never showed."

Heath couldn't believe this. "Something must have happened?" he speculated. "A car accident? An illness?"

Tara slowly shook her head. "He didn't pick up his phone...wouldn't answer his door. I worried about him for weeks. Then, eventually, one of our mutual friends told me what had happened. He'd gotten cold feet and moved back to Atlanta. He had a hometown girlfriend there from high school."

"Oh Tara, that's awful."

"Not for them." Moisture glistened in her eyes. "They've apparently got two kids now, and are very happy."

Heath laid his hand on Tara's coat sleeve, unable to imagine what Tara must have gone through during all that time when Ned had gone incommunicado. "He was a coward, Tara. I hope you know that. And not anywhere near good enough for you."

A smile trembled across her lips. "You're very sweet to say so."

"I'm not a sugary kind of guy," he told her honestly. "I call things as they are. And, you are..." He gently tightened his grip on her arm. "Pretty special."

Tara lowered her voice and said coyly, "Yeah well, so are you."

"Can I refill your glass?" he asked, glancing at the near-empty bottle.

"Just one more," she agreed. Then she playfully rolled her eyes. "Seeing as how I'm not driving."

"I'm glad that neither of us is traveling tonight." Heath topped off their drinks. "I'm fairly contented just sitting here with you."

"Yeah, me too." She took in the gorgeous panorama of the twinkling night sky and the light-studded buildings around them. "This is a far cry from Beaumont, Maine. I'll tell you that."

"What's it like there?" he prodded.

"I think you know." She grinned playfully. "I've certainly filled you in enough on my daily activities."

"I'll bet it's beautiful," he said. "I hear the tides are very dramatic."

"Oh yes! Incredible! And the seascapes are amazing, too."

"I'd like to see those someday," Heath said, pondering the possibility. He searched her eyes, seeing if she'd take the bait.

"That would be nice," she finally answered, after a silence that had him holding his breath.

"You could show me your bookshop. Take me around."

"Cook you some lobster."

"Now, *that* sounds tempting." He grinned broadly and she grinned back.

"Maybe sometime you can show me Savannah?"

"There's nothing I'd love more."

"Ever think of leaving?"

"You mean, permanently?" he asked, taken aback. "I don't see how I could. My business is there." After a quiet moment, he added, "So is my Granddad Lyle."

"You two must be close," she said intuitively.

"Yeah, very."

"Does he still live on his own?"

Heath shook his head. "He's in a retirement home, but it's a *really* nice one. They've got a movie theater...a bar..."

"A *bar*?" Tara interrupted with a musical laugh. "My, my. Sounds like quite a place!"

"Sure is," Heath said lightly. "They even offer travelers."

"Travelers?" Tara queried.

"Drinks to-go," he informed her. "It's very southern, and very Savannah. I think you'd like the city," he said, considering her. "You'd fit right in. You look just like a southern belle."

Tara raised an eyebrow. "With a good dose of Yankee attitude?"

Heath belly-laughed at this. "You, Tara, are too much fun to be around."

"You're not such bad company, either."

"Have you ever thought of leaving Maine?" he asked, mimicking her earlier query to him. "I mean, obviously, you went away to school in Louisiana."

"Yes, but now my life is there. In Beaumont. Plus, my dad's there, too. I'm all he's got. It would be hard to leave him."

"No brothers or sisters?"

Tara shook her head. "You mentioned you have a brother?"

"A younger one, yeah. Johnny works in financial consulting with my dad."

"And your mom?"

"She's an interior decorator."

"That sounds exciting."

"It is, for her. She loves it, and has become quite successful."

"That's great." Tara smiled brightly. "She sounds amazing."

"And, your mother? You didn't mention—?"

Tara's face fell and Heath instantly regretted asking the question. "She left years ago. So long ago I barely remember her, to tell you the truth."

Heath's heart ached for her. While his folks weren't perfect, they'd always stood together and had been a boon to his small family. They and his brother had consistently been there for Heath, and the support was mutual.

That's what family was. At least, how he interpreted it. His relationship with his Granddad Lyle was an added bonus, and he felt so glad to have him. Lyle thought the world of Heath, as well. That was one reason he'd asked him to take over his banking business. "I'm sorry to hear that, Tara. That sounds rough. For you and your dad, too."

"She ran away with a potter, I hear," Tara said disbelievingly. "Creative type. My dad is just the opposite. Terribly staid." She lowered her voice into a baritone when she said this and Heath couldn't help but smile.

"An old stick-in-the-mud?"

"In a way." She tilted her head to the side, and dark hair spilled over her shoulder. "He's in banking."

Heath bit back a laugh as wine zinged up his nose. "Really?" he asked, dabbing his mouth with a napkin.

"He doesn't run one like you," Tara offered quickly. "He's a teller at a local branch."

"Which bank?" Heath inquired politely.

"North Shore Central."

That did sound rather familiar, though it clearly wasn't one of the larger names.

"Have you heard of it?"

"Think so." Something tugged at the back of Heath's mind. He couldn't shake the sensation that he had, only he couldn't place where. "Is he happy there?"

"Oh, yes. He's spent his whole career at North Shore Central," Tara answered brightly. "He's told me many times he'd never work anywhere else."

****

An hour later, Heath walked Tara to her hotel room door. Oriental carpets lined the halls and long mirrors in ornate gold frames hung above Queen Anne style tables holding arrangements of fresh flowers. Tara felt almost like Dorothy, who'd arrived in the magical Land of Oz. Beaumont, Maine couldn't have felt farther away now than Kansas must have seemed to that little girl with pigtails and a dog named Toto.

While this realm wasn't filled with a wizard and witches, Tara nonetheless felt like she'd been transported to a magical place. She'd never had a man make her feel so special, and she'd clearly never experienced an elaborate first date like this.

Heath drew near and she caught a whiff of his spicy cologne. "Thanks for going out with me, and coming to New York." He cupped a hand to her cheek and her skin warmed beneath his touch. "I know it was a distance to travel..." His voice grew husky. "An imposition."

Tara moistened her impossibly parched lips, imagining the feel of his mouth on hers. "It was no trouble at all."

His dark brown gaze washed over her. "Will you see me again?"

"How about tomorrow for breakfast?"

He traced her lips with his thumb. "I meant, after that?"

Tara's heart raced as she imagined what that might entail. Her traveling to Savannah? Him coming to Maine? She couldn't fathom denying Heath anything, much less another date. "I'd like that," she said, smiling up at him.

She was hungry for him to kiss her, aching to feel his mouth on hers. "The dinner was wonderful. So was the show. Thank you."

He gave her a sexy grin and stepped closer. "Thank *you* for a wonderful day." The hand on her cheek slipped into her hair and his breath warmed her lips. "I can't recall a better one."

Her heart pounded and her face burned hot. "Me, either."

Heath's lips brushed over hers and her breath shuddered. "I'll call you when I get back to Savannah." The words were like a song to her heart as his mouth moved in. His kiss was sweet and strong, the pressure of his lips gently increasing until Tara found herself whimpering up against him. He slid his arms around her and held her close. "That's a promise," he said between satiny soft kisses, and Tara moaned in reply.

He kissed her more deeply then and Tara found herself being swept away. "Do you always keep your promises?" she asked, her breath ragged.

Heath pulled back and viewed her warmly. "Yes." The certainty with which he said it made Tara's heart dance. Her attraction to Heath wasn't one-sided.

He was clearly also very interested in her, and just as eager as she was for this relationship to continue. Perhaps Tara was setting herself up for heartache with a long-distance affair, but it was hard to fight the force of her heart when it battled with her head. Despite Tara's business savvy, when it came to her personal life, her emotions generally ruled.

"This could get complicated," she managed.

"I don't mind complicated." Heath shot her a tilted smile and her pulse quickened again. "Not when the complications are worth it."

Then he kissed her one last time and took her breath away.

Chapter Eleven

THE FOLLOWING SATURDAY, Tara found herself walking hand in hand with Heath through Forsyth Park beneath the broad promenade of live oaks dripping with Spanish moss and toward the north end's gurgling fountain. Lovers dotted park benches, nestled close together in the early morning chill, as Tara and Heath clutched their carryout cups of coffee. It was a gorgeous morning with sunlight streaming through the trees and gulls from the nearby ocean soaring through the clear blue sky. Heath had promised to take Tara out to Tybee Beach this afternoon and she was looking forward to the adventure.

Heath had met her plane at the airport, insisting on picking her up. Since she'd flown in from Boston after working a partial day at the bookshop, Tara hadn't arrived until after dinnertime. There'd still been enough of the night left for Heath to show her a bit of local color though. He'd taken her to a jazz club she found reminiscent of the ones she'd known in New Orleans. They'd ordered food there to go with their drinks, as she'd only had a snack on the plane and Heath hadn't eaten much of anything beforehand either.

After a fun evening out, she'd stayed in one of the nicely decorated guestrooms in Heath's impeccably restored turn-of-the-last-century town house. Its window overlooked a bricked-in backyard with a high ivy-covered wall and a large patio area, partially shaded by a formidable magnolia tree. Gardens were planted around the perimeter, housing gardenias, rhododendron, and camellias, interspersed with creeping ferns and pretty purple periwinkle ground cover. All were starting to fade from the recent frosts, but had apparently enjoyed a long autumn season.

Tara was grateful Heath had thought to provide her with separate accommodations, as well as pleased by his gentlemanly restraint. He clearly wasn't interested in rushing her, and Tara was happy to take things as they were moving along: at a leisurely pace, just as gentle and forgiving as the soft Savannah breeze.

"So," he asked, swinging their interlocked hands together. "What do you think of our fair city so far?"

"It's beautiful," she told him. "And very genteel. Lots of old-world charm here."

"Remind you of New Orleans?"

"In some ways. It's smaller, of course. But there's a similar European quality to this town, like there is there."

"I'll bet that was a fun place to go to college."

"Yeah, I enjoyed it."

"Have you ever returned?"

A torrent of hurt surged through her, and Tara beat the painful memories back. "I've never really thought about it."

Heath's face fell. "I'm sorry, Tara. I'm such a clod. I wasn't thinking. About your—"

"It's okay," she assured him. And, oddly, it was. Somehow, when Tara was with Heath, her relationship with Ned seemed like ancient history. Perhaps, because it was. "That was such a long time ago! Nearly ten years."

"Wow. That is a long time." He frowned pensively. "It hasn't even been ten *weeks* since my breakup with Caroline, but somehow that seems like eons ago."

"Are you sure you're okay with going back out to the beach?" He'd shared with her about his aborted attempt to propose, and the moment he'd found her bottle.

"Nothing would make me happier," Heath said surely. "I want you to see where I closed the book on one chapter in my life." He sweetly kissed her hand. "And a whole new story for me began."

"Thank you for planning this weekend," she told him. "I'm having such a great time."

"Thanks for agreeing to come here." Despite his earnest offer to foot the bill for her plane fare, Tara was proud she'd decided to pay her own way. Their first date in New York had been a sweeping opening gesture on Heath's part. Now, she wanted to put things back on more equal footing. Tara had even greater plans for that when she invited Heath to Maine. She hoped to get him to visit her in Beaumont soon, maybe even for Thanksgiving.

"Seems like a cool place to live," she said, glancing around the beautiful park.

"It is, and—believe it or not—an Irish Lass like you would actually be in good company."

"Yeah?"

"We've got our share of Irish heritage here." He motioned toward the fountain. "Every St. Patrick's Day that fountain's dyed green."

"Seriously?" Tara laughed with delight. "I had no idea."

"There's much more to learn about Savannah than can be gleaned in one weekend." He shared a telling look, and Tara directly met his gaze.

"That just means I'll have to come back."

Heath's laughter rumbled. "Indeed."

He released her hand, wrapping his arm around her shoulder. "I hope you'll return often."

****

Later that afternoon, they stood among the gusty winds of Tybee Beach. It was mid-November so the beach was nearly barren, with just a few evening surf fishers setting up their poles. "It's gorgeous out here," Tara said, observing the setting sun.

Heath grinned sexily. "Better today than I've ever seen it."

"There you go with your sweet talking, again." She playfully elbowed him as they strode through the sand. While it wasn't cold enough to warrant the full winter gear Tara wore in Maine, she definitely appreciated the windbreaker qualities of her mid-weight jacket. Heath had his jacket zipped up, too, yet his hands were bare while she had donned a scarf and gloves.

"I only tell you nice things because I mean them."

"Yeah well, I appreciate them. I really do." She cut him a sideways glance and grinned. "I'd much rather have you complimenting me than anyone else."

"Sweetheart," he said, and her cheeks flushed at the endearment. "There *is* nobody else. Hasn't been since I unleashed that genie from its bottle." He winked then stopped walking. "We're here." His hand swept over the shore, gesturing toward the water. "This was the place of my undoing."

Tara laughed lightly at this. "Oh, yeah?"

"Yeah." He took her in his arms and kissed her soundly. Winds gusted around them, turning over small shells and ruffling through Tara's hair.

She brought her palms to his cheeks and met Heath's gaze. "Well, *this* is the place of *my* undoing."

His brow rose questioningly.

"Right here in your arms," she said with a saucy edge.

A slow grin warmed his face. "What time does your plane leave tomorrow?"

"Three o'clock. Why?"

"I was thinking I'd take you for shrimp and grits at my favorite brunch place, before making a stop on our way to the airport."

"Oh? Where are we going?"

He hugged her up against him and kissed the top of her head. "Someplace special. You'll see."

Chapter Twelve

THE NEXT AFTERNOON, Tara was surprised to find Heath showing his credentials to a guard at a gated retirement community. Then she remembered Heath's stated affection for his paternal grandfather, and it all made sense.

"I hope you don't mind the detour?" he said, driving them past the gatehouse. "There's someone I'd really like you to meet."

"I'd be honored," Tara said, meaning it absolutely. It touched her deeply that Heath wanted her to meet someone so significant to him.

He parked his car then led her through the entrance of a grand old building with a lushly manicured lawn and towering ivory columns on either side of its stately front door. The nurses in the reception area greeted Heath cheerily. He was apparently a regular figure around here, as everyone knew his name, though they addressed him very formally as Mr. Wellington when they said *good afternoon.* A charge nurse named Martha with short blond curls turned his way and smiled. "He's in the atrium," she offered, indicating the whereabouts of Heath's grandfather. "We're having music there this afternoon."

As they approached that area, chords of classical music echoed down the expansive hallway toward them. Tara discerned various string instruments: a violin, a viola, a double bass, and maybe a cello. They paused on the threshold to a room with a vaulted glass ceiling and pretty potted plants all around, and Heath waved an older gentleman's way.

Lyle Wellington's face lit up, as he pivoted his wheelchair toward them with a smile. He backed his automated chair away from the crowd that had gathered to hear the talented string ensemble, and quietly glided toward them. Tara was struck by the similarities in his and Heath's appearances. While his face was older and etched with wrinkles, they shared a resemblance and Heath's dark chocolate-brown eyes.

"Heath, my boy," he said, clasping Heath's hand between both of his. "What an unexpected pleasure."

"I tried phoning this morning," Heath explained. "But you weren't in your room."

"Probably on a date with one of the pretty nurses," Lyle joked, winking at Tara, and she laughed warmly. "Who's this charming young lady?" he asked his grandson.

"Granddad, I'd like you to meet Tara McAdams."

She extended her hand, and Lyle took it, squeezing it firmly in his. "It's a pleasure, my dear."

"It's so nice to meet you, too," Tara told him. "Heath's said so many nice things about you."

"Has he, now?" Lyle brought his hand to his chin to study Heath. "That must mean you're after something. Come on now, what is it?"

Heath chuckled good-naturedly. "Granddad, you know that's not true." He gripped the handlebars on the wheelchair and steered them toward a more private spot. Tara saw he was aiming for a small seating area in an adjoining room.

Lyle stared back at Heath over his shoulder. "Oh yes, it is." Next, he addressed Tara. "The last time he was nice to me, I gave him my bank."

Tara giggled at this and Heath sighed. "That's right," he said cajolingly. "I wheedled it right out from under you."

"He might have, at that," Lyle confided to Tara. "That is, if I hadn't determined him as the best man for the job first."

Heath positioned the wheelchair beside the sofa and Lyle asked both him and Tara to please take a seat. As Tara did, Lyle questioned, "You're not from Savannah, I take it?"

"No, sir. But how did you—?"

"A girl as pretty as you wouldn't have escaped my grandson's notice for this long. Not unless he was being a really big dummy." He quizzically eyed Heath. "You weren't, were you?"

"Granddad..."

"It's all right," Tara said, laughing. "And no, Mr. Wellington, I can assure you that Heath has actually been very smart. He took me on an incredibly romantic first date, in fact."

Heath sat up a little straighter in his palmetto chair, apparently liking the sound of Tara praising him to his grandfather.

"Is that so?" Lyle leaned toward Heath with interest. "Where'd you go?"

"To New York City." He tried to downplay it, but Tara detected a note of accomplishment underneath. "For coffee, dinner, and a show."

Lyle opened his mouth to speak but Heath stopped him. "Separate rooms."

"Well, good." The old man leaned back in his chair satisfied. "Not that I'm really that old-fashioned."

"Not that it's really any of your business," Heath bantered.

"You offered," Lyle countered.

"Because, I knew if I didn't, you'd ask."

Lyle raised his brow at Tara and spoke behind the back of his hand. "Is he always this pesky with you?"

She chuckled merrily, appreciating the camaraderie Heath and Lyle clearly enjoyed. "Only sometimes."

"Hey!" Heath protested, but he was grinning.

"In any case," Tara said primly, crossing her legs. "You'll be happy to know Heath was the perfect gentleman. And..." She grinned coyly. "He swept me off my feet."

Tara wasn't sure, but she thought she detected a hint of color beneath Heath's open collar. He wore a golf shirt under a sweater and khakis with loafers. The outfit was casual but polished and suited him to a tee. It certainly didn't hurt that he was the best-looking guy she'd seen. Ever.

Heath's dark brown eyes locked on hers. "That was the plan."

Lyle grinned broadly and clapped his hands together. "Heath's always been an excellent planner. That's one reason he's so good at his job."

"Sounds like you did a phenomenal job starting the bank that Heath took over," Tara commented.

"Yes, but it was a small-potatoes operation back in the day. Nothing like it is now." He admiringly viewed his grandson. "Heath's brought it a long way."

"Tara's dad is in banking," Heath said.

"That so?" Lyle asked, his interest piqued. "Whereabouts?"

"Up in Beaumont, Maine," Tara said. "It's a very small bank. I'm sure you haven't heard of it."

"Try me."

"North Shore Central."

Lyle thumped his fingers against his armrest. "Nope, don't believe I have, but that doesn't mean much. I've been out of the business for some time. Heath, on the other hand..." He turned Heath's way, and Heath nodded.

"I have heard of it, yes. I just can't recall the context. I've been meaning to look it up at work."

"Do you think we've had dealings?" Lyle questioned.

"Sometime in the past?" Heath questioned. "It's possible."

Tara wasn't so sure. When she'd mentioned Heath's bank to her dad, he'd naturally heard of it, since it had grown into such a large entity. But he hadn't mentioned anything beyond that. After returning from New York, Tara had filled her dad in on her relationship with Heath in a general way. Richard hadn't been thrilled about Tara sending a message in a bottle, and he remained skeptical about her involvement with some big businessman from the south. The fact that Heath was also in banking didn't necessarily seem to help. Tara hoped her dad's opinion of Heath would soften a bit once the two men met face to face.

"Is that where you live?" Lyle asked Tara, referring back to her mention of Beaumont, Maine.

Tara beamed happily. "Yes, it is."

"Tara went to college in New Orleans," Heath informed Lyle. "So, she's not a total stranger to the south."

Lyle chuckled warmly. "Didn't imagine she was." He eyed Tara admiringly. "She looks just like Scarlett O'Hara."

Tara blushed deeply, because this wasn't the first time she'd heard the comparison. Her old boyfriend, Ned, used to say that a lot. Though Ned had nothing at all in common with Rhett Butler. *A certain banker gentleman from Savannah, however…*Tara thought, her mind starting to wander.

"She does favor Vivien Leigh in that movie, doesn't she?" Heath observed with surprise. "Although, in my opinion, Tara's much prettier."

"Guys!" Tara cried, feeling fire in her cheeks.

"Plus, she's a heck of a lot sweeter," Heath told his granddad with conviction. "Tara's every bit as smart as Scarlett was, and savvy in business. But Tara's not conniving in any way. She didn't have to use her feminine wiles or employ underhanded tactics to catch my eye."

Lyle clucked his tongue. "Well, well. I guess that says it all." He bowed his chin at Tara. "My hat's off to you. I've never heard my grandson speak that way about anyone."

Heath uncomfortably cleared his throat, perhaps wondering if he'd gone too far. But Tara didn't think he had. She'd loved and appreciated every heartfelt word. "We should probably get going," he said, shooting Tara a glance. When she confirmed with a nod, he added, "Tara's got a flight out of Savannah this afternoon."

"Leaving, already?" Lyle's forehead rose plaintively. "I'm so sorry, dear. It seems we've barely met."

Tara got to her feet then assured him, "I'll be back."

Lyle grinned at Heath, then at Tara. "Fantastic. When?"

"We'll work it out, and I'll tell you," Heath said, giving Lyle's shoulder a pat.

"I'll look forward to it," Lyle told Tara with a smile.

****

Heath arrived at his office on Monday more determined than ever to learn more about North Shore Central. It was important to him, because it was important to Tara. She was obviously very devoted to her father, and he'd worked there for years. While in some ways the fact that it had been in operation so long made North Shore Central sound stable, Heath was seasoned enough to know that wasn't necessarily the case. A lot of smaller banks were going under. He knew this firsthand from the number of failing entities he'd had to rescue by absorbing their assets under his larger corporate wing. It was hard to compete in today's global economy with the limited assets afforded the more modest institutions.

He looked North Shore Central up online and was struck by the familiarity of its logo. Heath reasoned he'd come across it before; he just couldn't put his finger on where... Then a small light bulb went on in a very dark corner of his brain. Before he knew it, it was blazing like the rising sun. "Kristin," he said, pressing the intercom buzzer on his desk. "Can you bring me the Chancellor file?"

The moment she did, Heath found himself flipping through its pages, even before his assistant had left the room. Each targeted financial institution was already failing and in a state of near-foreclosure. Whether or not they'd shared this dire financial forecast with their existing employees or current stockholders was beyond Heath's control, and anybody's guess. The individual bank files were secured by paperclips and arranged in alphabetical order. When

Heath got to the *N*s, his heart caught in his throat. North Shore Central in Beaumont, Maine, was among the dozens of banks to be put out of business by the end of the year.

Chapter Thirteen

TARA COULDN'T WAIT for Heath to visit Beaumont. Though he'd seemed a bit more preoccupied during their daily phone calls, he'd said that was because he'd been extra busy at work. When Tara had issued her invitation, he'd accepted without reservation, and she'd been overjoyed at the prospect of Heath spending Thanksgiving in Maine. She'd initially worried he wouldn't want to leave his grandfather, but he'd explained that his mom and dad still arranged to take Lyle to Charlotte for their family gathering each year. Heath was certain the rest of the Wellingtons could carry on without him. In fact, he'd guessed that his granddad would insist on as much. Lyle was plenty taken with Tara, and had made no bones about saying so to Heath.

"I loved meeting your granddad, too," she said happily into the receiver. Heath had phoned shortly after her store's opening to double-check with Tara regarding his arrival time later today. He planned to fly into Boston and rent a car from there.

"What can I bring you from Savannah?"

"I didn't see any when I was there, but I assume you can find pralines?"

"I know a candy shop on River Street that makes them."

"Will you bring us a box? My dad would find that a treat. I used to bring those to him from New Orleans," she continued. "He could never get enough!"

Heath laughed in understanding. "Anything else?"

"Just you." Tara sighed contentedly. "I can't believe you're really coming. I can't wait to show you around."

"I'm looking forward to it."

"We're expecting more snow. Dress warmly."

"I will." He hesitated a moment before asking, "Tara? Are you sure about the accommodations? I seriously don't mind booking a hotel."

"There *are no* hotels in Beaumont, I've told you." She giggled happily. "You're absolutely staying with me."

"But your place is small. You said so yourself."

"I've got a futon."

"Sounds very...inviting."

"Stop sounding like a pouty child," she scolded. "If you don't want it, I'll sleep there and you can take my bed."

"How about we work that out once I get there?"

"Sounds like a plan." But the image that kept playing in Tara's mind involved Heath snuggled up with her on the futon in her cozy apartment. With snow lightly pinging against the windows and a fire blazing in her woodstove. Tara sighed heavily, realizing she'd been daydreaming ever since ending her call with Heath.

"Going to be that good, huh?" Jeannie asked from behind the checkout counter.

"Shut up."

"I know you were mooning over him," Jeannie said, "and thinking about his visit." She pointedly arched an eyebrow. "There's going to be a hot time in the old town tonight!"

"He's sleeping on the futon."

"Right."

"Jean-nie!" In spite of herself, Tara's cheeks colored.

"I'm just saying... It gets awfully cold in Maine this time of year."

"Which is why I'm picking up extra logs for the woodstove."

"Maybe you won't need the fire to keep you warm." Jeannie winked and Tara groaned.

"Spoken like a woman in love."

"Takes one to know one," Jeannie replied smartly.

****

By the time Heath landed in Boston, it was snowing hard. He'd rented an SUV in anticipation of the weather, and now navigated the interstate that would take him into Maine. It was the Wednesday before Thanksgiving, and the roads were crowded, with traffic moving along at a snail's pace. Once Heath cleared Massachusetts and got into New Hampshire, driving conditions improved. When he reached Maine and the exit to the much smaller rural highway that led toward Augusta, traffic thinned even more. Heath drove for miles without spotting another vehicle, his wiper blades sweeping hard against the pounding snow. There were no streetlights here, and the sky was charcoal gray fading to black, its color darkening above torrents of snow as night moved in.

Heath had spent the past ten days trying to reconcile the situation with North Shore Central, but, despite his inquiries, he hadn't been able to learn much from the bank's current proprietors. He supposed they viewed Wellington International as the enemy, and Heath could understand why. If only they'd talk to him, he hoped to ensure a smoother transition.

While Wellington International strove to keep as many of the original employees in place during any bank takeover, some fallout was inevitable as Wellington management would naturally be put in place. Since Tara's father was a teller, Heath wanted to believe that his position would be spared. Ultimately, it was up to the home bank to make the cuts among its own people. Wellington simply supplied the new management team and let the acquisition bank take care of the rest. *In other words, do their dirty work*, Heath thought with a hint of shame.

He'd never really viewed his bank as the villain. His corporation saved businesses that were failing. Rather than having an entire bank shut down and lose all of its people, when Wellington came in, the bank could continue to thrive—only with a new nameplate on its door, and with minimal impact on its original staff. Some impact was there, though. There was no denying that. But, up until now, none of it had seemed quite so personal.

Heath hadn't mentioned any of this to Tara, as he hadn't wanted to concern her. He also wasn't sure how much her father knew about the precarious state of the bank where he worked. Had the higher-ups at North Shore Central even bothered to share with their employees what was coming? Or, were they leaving this as a holiday surprise, to be sprung on affected workers in mid-December, giving them no more than the required two weeks' notice? This seemed highly unfair, particularly because, as Tara had told him, most of those people had been in their positions at North Shore Central for years. Some of them, like her father, had been there their entire careers.

While Heath hadn't been able to make headway with his inquiries to date, he still had until the end of the year to try to improve the situation for Tara's dad. Or, at least, feel assured that Richard's particular job wasn't at stake. For this reason, he decided to keep quiet on the matter, unless Tara's father had already caught wind of the takeover, and decided to bring it up first.

Chapter Fourteen

TARA RACED DOWN the steps of her upstairs apartment when she saw Heath's headlights in the drive. The moment he stepped from the door of his SUV, she sprang toward him, leaping into his arms. Heath laughed heartily and lifted her up in a hug, holding her against his chest as he swung her around in the driving snow. He gazed up at her, dark eyes shining, his wavy dark hair rapidly becoming covered by snow.

"Welcome to Maine, I guess?"

"Yes!" She planted her palms on his cheeks and kissed his lips firmly. "Welcome to Beaumont, Heath!"

He chuckled again then slowly set her down on the gravel drive, which crunched beneath her boot heels. "Now, that's a welcoming party I can appreciate."

Tara grinned and glanced back in his SUV through the driver's door that remained ajar. "Can I help you with your things?"

"Don't have much," he said. "Just a backpack and a carry-on." He stared down at her open winter parka. Tara had dashed out the door so quickly, she hadn't taken time to zip it. "You must be freezing. Let's get you back inside."

"Grab your things," she instructed cheerily. "We'll go together."

Tara felt as happy as a child on Christmas morning. Heath had come to see her in Maine, and she was about to show him her domain. She so hoped he'd like it. Tara had worked extra hard to make her tiny apartment cozy, by adding surplus firewood and vases of fresh flowers. She'd also purchased scented candles, which she'd placed strategically around the rooms.

There were really only three of them: the main living area with the futon, which opened on a galley kitchen with a window overlooking the bay; her miniscule bathroom, which was no bigger than a closet; and the modest bedroom that barely accommodated her double bed, two end tables, and a wooden hope chest, in which she stored extra blankets. There wasn't ample area in her bedroom for a dresser, so she kept her underclothing in stacking bins at the bottom of her closet and hung the rest of her clothes above them in the jam-packed space.

It was simple, but it was home. Plus, the woodstove functioned properly, and you couldn't beat the rent. The view from the kitchen window was pretty fantastic, too.

****

Heath took in the exterior of the converted barn and the broad snowy field beyond it leading to the darkened bay. "Bet it's beautiful out here in daylight."

"Wait until you see it in the morning."

He nabbed his suitcase and backpack from the hatchback, slinging the backpack over his shoulder. With his free hand, he took Tara's. Her fingers were chilly, wrapping around his, but her touch made him warm all over. Heath had never enjoyed holding hands with a woman as much. Mostly, he enjoyed the tangible connection of them being together. He found Tara's presence sweet and reassuring, in a very womanly and companionable way.

She led him through the barn door where he saw straw strewn about on an earthen floor and bound bales of hay off to one side with some old farm equipment, including an ancient tractor that looked like it hadn't been driven in years.

"This way!" she beckoned with a smile. Tara opened a narrow door on the far wall and cheerfully tugged him toward a wooden staircase. He could tell she was excited about him being here, and her joy was contagious. Not that Heath wasn't already feeling pretty great about the situation himself. All the way here, he'd fretted over that dreadful bank business, but the moment he'd seen Tara, his worries had melted away. He'd work things out, of course he would. That's what Heath did, and who he was: a fixer. Very skilled at setting things right.

They reached the landing at the top of the stairs, entering the charming second-floor apartment. It was furnished simply but in good taste, and there were many thoughtful touches throughout. Fresh flower arrangements stood on tables, and ornamental candles burned softly beside framed photos of Tara with different people Heath assumed to be her friends, and her father. There was even one of a group of women standing on a beach somewhere. "Aha!" he exclaimed, eyeing the photo. "Enchanted Island?"

"Yes. That was taken at the fancy resort where we stayed." She pointed at another framed photo across the way. "That other one over there is of me with my dad." Tara's cheeks glowed in the candlelight, making her appear lovelier than ever. "And, this one's of me and Jeannie," she said, indicating a picture showing her with a freckled blonde. Both smiled brightly into the camera and shelves of books stood behind them.

"Was that taken in your shop?" Heath inquired.

Tara beamed proudly. "I can't wait to show it to you."

"I can't wait to see it. I don't believe I've ever been to a romance-only bookstore before."

She twisted her lips to study him then burst into giggles. "No, I don't suppose you have. Well, there's always a first time!"

Heath surveyed the room, trying to decide where to set down his luggage.

"Oh!" Tara said, apparently reading him. "Please. Why don't you put your things in there?" She motioned through an open door into another room. Through it, Heath spied the end of what looked like a double bed.

"Isn't that your room?"

"I told you I was taking the futon," Tara replied stubbornly.

"And I told you I wouldn't let you do that."

"No," she countered quickly. "You said we'd work things out when you got here. And, now we have!"

She grinned like it was settled, and Heath indulgently shook his head.

"We *will* work this out later," he said, waggling a finger in her direction, before carting his bags into her room. He set his things down beside the bed, then returned to the living area to find Tara uncorking some wine. Two pots simmered on the stove, and the oven light was on. Heath detected the delectable aromas of garlic, spices, and savory shellfish.

"I thought you might like wine with your dinner?"

He immediately recognized the label and grinned. "Seems like that's becoming our signature drink."

"If you'd like something else—?" she asked nervously.

"No, no! That Chianti is great. It came highly recommended to me by a very knowledgeable wine connoisseur I know."

Tara smiled at this.

"You'd probably like to remove your coat and use the restroom," she observed. Heath noted she'd already hung her parka on a hook by the top of the stairs. He hung his coat up as well, then answered, "I would like to wash my hands, if you'll just point the way?"

She nodded over her shoulder at what looked like a small coat closet.

"In there?" he asked, amazed.

"Everything fits!" she responded lightly. "It's just very tight."

Heath chuckled then pulled back the door, seeing Tara was right. A pint-size pedestal sink sidled up to the smallest shower stall he'd ever seen. At the end of the narrow room, and tucked under the downward sloping ceiling, stood a toilet. He'd have to duck his head to use it. But that was okay. Heath had the notion he was going to feel very at home here.

****

Heath returned a few minutes later, noting that Tara had everything under control. The dinner was almost ready, and seemed to be coming along perfectly.

"What's cooking?" He drew near and wrapped his arms around her from behind.

"My homemade lobster ravioli and homemade garlic bread."

Heath set his chin on her shoulder. "Smells delicious."

"I was hoping you would like it." She smiled back at him. "Plus, it goes with the wine."

"You know," he said in a low voice. "If I didn't know better, I'd swear you were Italian, not Irish."

"I am!" She grinned sassily. "But only half. On my mother's side." Tara liked to think if her mom had left her nothing else, she'd somehow imbued in her the love of Italian cooking. Tara was pleased to be quite good at it. Her friends always raved about her culinary talents, though she didn't have the opportunity to cook for others often.

Her dad wouldn't eat Italian. It was a matter of pride, or hurt, or disappointment. Tara wasn't sure which, but she understood the cuisine reminded Richard of her mother, Sophia. So she never pressed him on it. Tara had plenty of friends with whom she could eat spaghetti, including Jeannie.

"A double-whammy!" Heath proclaimed, nibbling her ear. "Half Irish and half Italian! No wonder I can't resist you."

"Now, stop," she scolded, but she was giggling. "I'll burn the bread."

He kissed her lightly on the cheek. "What can I do to help?"

"Set the table and put on the salads. They're already fixed and in the fridge."

He reluctantly released her and complied.

"I'm looking forward to meeting your dad tomorrow."

"He's looking forward to meeting you, too," Tara lied. The truth was she'd had to force her father to accept the fact that Heath was coming to dinner, whether he liked it or not. She'd also made Richard swear to be on his best behavior. *None of this "corporate America is destroying the rest of the world" talk, Dad. Please.*

"But I'm especially looking forward to this dinner tonight."

"Thank you."

"Thank you for inviting me to Maine. I love your place, and what you've done with it."

"I found your townhome pretty spectacular myself."

"Yes," he said pensively. "But now that I've seen your apartment, I've decided it's been missing something."

Tara slid on her oven mitts and withdrew the steaming, aromatic garlic bread from the oven. "Oh? What's that?"

Heath shot her a warm grin. "You."

"I've said it before and I'll say it again, you really are a charmer."

"If you say so," he said, returning to the kitchen. She served a couple of plates and handed them to him. The perfectly formed pasta bites in a heavenly lobster cream sauce looked divine.

"This is gourmet cooking," he said, carrying the plates to the table.

"Only the best for my Savannah gent," she said with a smile.

****

A little while later, the two of them snuggled together on the futon by the glowing woodstove, as snow gently fell outside the windows. Tara had covered them with a throw blanket and refreshed their glasses of wine. Heath brought an arm around her, thinking he'd never felt more at peace than he did right now. There was no boardroom business to consider, or busy travel schedule to adhere to. *All I have to do is sit here and relax with the woman I lov...* He choked on his wine, reality hitting him upside the head.

"Heath? What is it? What's wrong?" Tara viewed him with concern, and he wiped the back of his mouth with his hand.

"I...um...was just thinking about how great it is to be with you."

She gave him a wry smile. "Kind of chokes you up, doesn't it?"

Heath chuckled warmly, thinking that was just one of the many things he loved about Tara: her sense of humor. And, he *did* love her, he could see that clearly now. She'd gotten to him in a way no other woman had. It was a new feeling. *Phenomenal.* He'd of course understood love objectively, and had even believed himself to be in it once or twice. Now, Heath saw he'd been wrong. He'd never known an emotion this deep and pure.

It made him want to hold onto Tara tightly, and never let her go. What's more, it made him want to give her the world. He set down his wine and hers, wrapping his arms around her.

She gazed up at him with her beautiful green eyes. "I was only joking, you know."

Heath lightly kissed her lips. "I know. I love it when you tease me. No other woman... What I mean is, you're very sure of yourself, Tara, but in such a great way. You're not stuck-up or pretentious. Just wonderful and real."

"I think you're pretty wonderful, too."

"I like the way we fit together. We're both so different and yet—"

Color warmed her cheeks. "It works."

"Sometimes the best things in life are long shots," he told her. "Spectacular doesn't come around every day."

"No," she said softly, and he kissed her again.

The fire crackled beside them as snow pinged against the windows, and shadows hugged the walls with candles burning low. He ran his fingers through her hair, cradling her head in his hands. "Tara, I have a confession to make..." When he drew nearer he whispered, "I've fallen madly...passionately...and *desperately* in love with you."

She viewed him tenderly, her lips quivering. "And, you've completely captured my heart." Then, she said the words he'd longed to hear. "I love you, Heath."

"Oh Tara," he said before claiming her mouth with his, "I love you too."

Chapter Fifteen

THE NEXT AFTERNOON, they stood on the covered front porch of Tara's father's house. It was a cute clapboard bungalow with cedar shake shingles set near the edge of town. Smoke coiled from its stone chimney, and light warmed its interior rooms.

Dusk fell as winds ripped off the nearby cove, chilling the air. Tara had shown Heath around Beaumont, and he'd loved seeing the quaint shops, the one local market, the post office and smallish library. There were a few churches, too, as well as a number of private homes, old houses that had been converted to art galleries, and other stores. One of them was Tara's bookstore, the Happy Hearts Bookshop.

While, naturally, everything was closed today, Heath had been able to get a sense of the tiny town and its tightly knit community. Particularly as Tara had shared personal anecdotes about the various shop owners and the residents she knew well. She'd also let him into her bookstore for a private tour, and he'd been very impressed with the place. He could tell she'd loved showing it off, too.

Tara's business was her pride and joy and she'd built it from the ground up. In the beginning, some folks had been skeptical, thinking a store specializing in romance novels couldn't possibly survive in this small town. Tara had been incredibly pleased to prove the naysayers wrong. Though she'd indicated that sales had been slow lately, Tara exuded confidence they would pick back up again soon. Christmas was coming, after all.

"Remember what I told you," Tara instructed, her breath clouding the air. "And, please don't take anything my dad says too seriously."

"I'm sure he's not the ogre you make him out to be," Heath whispered hoarsely as she rang the bell.

Tara held a sweet potato casserole in her hands, and Heath carried the wine and a gift box of pralines. They'd brought a Merlot and a Sauvignon Blanc, in order to give them all a choice. Chianti was their special couple wine, and Tara's dad wasn't a huge fan of Italian food or drink, anyway.

Richard McAdams pulled back the door with a broad smile, but his good nature was directed at his daughter. "Tara, my dear! Happy Thanksgiving!" The barrel-chested man with silvery hair and a short solid frame hugged Tara briefly.

When he turned his coal-black eyes on Heath, some of that warmth evaporated. "You must be the young man Tara's told me about." He extended a hand and Heath shifted the bottles in his grasp to shake it.

"It's nice meeting you, Mr. McAdams."

He shooed them both inside and quickly shut the door against the howling winds at their backs. "Please, call me Richard." While he was being polite, there was stiffness in his demeanor. Heath somehow had the notion that Tara had told her dad to be on his best behavior, and he appeared to be trying. "Thanks for bringing the wine and the candies," he said when Heath handed him the gift box.

"They're Savannah pralines," Heath offered. "Tara said you might enjoy them."

"Probably not as much as the ones from New Orleans."

"*Dad*," Tara hissed sharply in low tones. "You're being rude." Then she straightened her spine and did her best to change the subject.

"It smells awesome in here," she said, slipping out of her coat. She took Heath's wine and set it on the entrance table along with her casserole, so he could remove his as well.

"Something does smell mighty good," Heath agreed. Then, he addressed Richard. "Thanks for including me in your Thanksgiving."

Richard grumbled something unintelligible and Tara gaped at him.

Heath awkwardly cleared his throat. "Should I take this wine to the kitchen?"

"Yes, let's!" Tara said, fiercely turning her back on her dad. She picked up her casserole, leading the way down the short hall. "Don't mind him," she said quietly. "He'll soften."

Heath sure hoped so. Otherwise, he was going to be in for a very long meal.

"Didn't mean that the way it sounded!" Richard called after them.

No, Heath thought. *You probably meant it worse*. Tara had shared that her dad was overprotective of his only child. He also harbored unwarranted suspicions about big businessmen and their secret motives, according to Tara. Heath had two strikes against him right out of the gate.

If Richard knew the truth about Wellington International's plans for North Shore Central, things would look even worse. That's why Heath intended to keep any mention of that acquisition totally off the Thanksgiving table.

They entered the cute kitchen with a white ceramic sink and gingham curtains hanging over its adjacent window. Though the kitchen was small, its décor was impeccable, with upscale stainless steel appliances complementing the sleek kitchen faucet and brushed chrome drawer pulls on Williamsburg blue cabinets. Lattice-glass doors showcased pretty blue and white china stacked on shelves, and the countertop was a marble-patterned granite. "Impressive kitchen," Heath remarked, setting down the wine.

A fully roasted turkey sat on the cooktop, while pots simmered on the other burners on the stove. Tara slid her casserole in the oven with another dish to keep it warm.

"My dad remodeled just last year," she offered. "He really loves to cook."

"I had to take out a big home equity loan to pay for it," Richard interrupted from the doorway. "But, it's been worth it, every cent."

"Your contractor did an incredible job."

"No contractor." Richard beamed proudly. "Did most of the work myself."

Heath's estimation of Richard grew. He always appreciated people who could do things for themselves. "That's amazing."

"Tara did the wiring."

"Wiring?" Heath viewed Tara with surprise and she laughed.

"He means, I put in the dimmer switch." She winked and pointed to an artsy chrome lamp hanging above the rustic kitchen table with four chairs. Heath saw it was set for dinner, with a paper, fan-out turkey in its center.

Richard caught Heath's eye on the decoration and said, "Tara made that when she was seven, you know. She always did have a thing for turk—"

"Dad!" Tara yelped and Richard's temples reddened. He turned his dark eyes on Heath's.

"Sorry," he said, sounding abashed. "Sometimes I can't help myself." He shrugged apologetically. "She *is* my only daughter."

"I don't blame you one bit, sir," Heath said. "I'd feel exactly the same if she were mine."

A companionable sheen glowed in Richard's eyes. "That so, lad?"

"Yes, sir."

"Then, come on, and let's have ourselves a drink."

"I'll open the wine," Tara offered.

"Forget your wine!" Richard said with a wave of his hand. He leaned toward Heath conspiratorially. "Who needs wine when we've got Irish whiskey, eh?"

****

The dinner seemed to go a lot better than Heath expected. He wasn't sure whether that was because he'd managed to form some sort of bond with Richard, or if he should thank the Irish whiskey. Just like Tara, Richard was an accomplished cook. The turkey was tender and delicious and its accompanying oyster stuffing was out of this world. Tara's sweet potato casserole was a hit, as was her dad's famous corn pudding. They had a chilled asparagus salad on the side, cranberry sauce, and rolls, with Richard's homemade pecan pie for dessert.

"Everything was fabulous," Heath said, as they finished up. "Thank you so much."

Richard cheerily tipped his tumbler to one side. "Thank you for being our guest!"

Tara smiled happily at Heath, and he could tell she was relieved that dinner had been a success. "It's been my honor to be here. Now, in return, I hope you'll let me do the dishes."

"Not yet!" Richard stopped him before he could stand. "First, we have a little something to celebrate!"

Heath and Tara glanced curiously at each other.

"Stay put," her dad instructed, then he retrieved a bottle from the freezer compartment of the refrigerator. "This should be nice and cold by now." Richard pulled three champagne flutes from a cabinet and returned to the table with those nested in one hand and a champagne bottle in the other.

Tara watched him wide-eyed. "Da-ad? What exactly are you doing?"

"Celebrating!" Richard replied heartily. He rejoined them at the table and set everything down, before surveying his remodeling handiwork in the room. "I thought it was going to take me five years to pay off the materials! Now, I'll get it done in two!"

Tara gaped at him, completely lost. "I'm not sure I understand?"

"It's my job, girl!" Richard stated happily. "Don't you know?" He stared proudly at his daughter and then shot a wink at Heath. "Just yesterday morning, I was promoted to branch manager. Just think! Twenty years in the same slot, and nothing! And, here I am in my ripe old middle age, getting advanced to the job of my dreams."

Chapter Sixteen

HEATH'S STOMACH FELT sour all the way back to Tara's apartment. What an underhanded trick for North Shore Central to play. By promoting Richard to management, they'd essentially sealed his fate in getting canned from the bank. Rather than having the guts to tell him outright that his job was in jeopardy, they'd staged this little charade of making him feel like a king for a day, only to have his throne yanked right out from beneath him.

The irony was, if they'd left Richard in his current teller position, his spot might have been spared. Heath wondered if someone at the bank secretly had it out for Richard, or whether he was simply a sacrificial lamb? If Richard was axed, that meant someone else could keep his or her job. Perhaps somebody who had temporarily been "demoted"... Hmm.

"You're being awfully quiet!" Tara said. Since she knew the area best, she'd offered to drive to her dad's house, which was fine with Heath. She'd been chauffeuring him around all day; Tara had stated he'd done enough driving coming in from Boston, and he hadn't wanted to argue with her.

"Just thinking over the great time I had," Heath replied. "Your dad is a really nice guy."

"I know he's a great, gruff grizzly sometimes, but he's really a teddy bear underneath."

"He certainly seems to have a soft side when it comes to you," Heath said sympathetically.

"Thanks for being so understanding, and for not letting him get to you."

"Tara, I—"

"What is it?" She turned toward him and her brow rose in concern. A raccoon skittered across their path, and Tara had to quickly apply the brakes.

"I think you'd better keep your eyes on the road."

"Of course." She tightened her gloved fingers around the steering wheel. "But something is bothering you, isn't it?" she asked intuitively.

"Bank business," he answered truthfully. "Nothing that can be addressed tonight."

"Then let's not worry about it tonight," she said resolutely. "You can worry about it when you get back to Savannah."

Heath eyed her lovely profile, knowing that he'd be worrying plenty. He had to find a way to fix this mess of a situation with her dad. At the same time, Heath understood that some of it was beyond his control. It was like a giant snowball had begun rolling, which was now gaining momentum. And, in the end, it was going to completely flatten the parent Tara worshiped: her dad. "All right," Heath agreed, trying to focus on something more positive. "What are our plans for the rest of the night?"

"Well, I have an idea..." Tara giggled impishly. "That might involve the futon."

Heath belly-laughed, finding her directness a turn-on. While they'd done nothing but kiss, they'd kissed a lot, and Tara's kisses had been extra hot. Heath had insisted on sleeping on the futon, because he really didn't mind, and ultimately she'd relented. "You keep this up, I'm never going to want to leave Maine."

She shot him a shy smile. "That's kind of what I was hoping."

****

Sunday morning in her driveway, Heath kissed Tara with a passion that made her fear she was never going to see him again. They'd shared a marvelous weekend together, and despite the snowy weather Tara had gotten to show Heath more of Beaumont. She'd also spent plenty of time snuggling with him indoors, and they'd made some incredibly romantic memories in her apartment.

"I'm going to miss you so much," he said, gazing into her eyes.

"And I'll miss you," she returned, from the depths of her soul.

"When can I see you again?" he asked. "Please tell me before Christmas?"

Her lips trembled in a smile, because that was her wish, too. "Will you come here?"

"If I can arrange it." He squared his shoulders with determination. "What I mean is, I *will* arrange it— just as soon as I can. I'll call."

"Good," she said, as her heart took wing. "I'll answer."

His lips pulled up in a smile. "Have you thought about what you want for Christmas?"

"Not yet," she said sunnily. "How about you?"

"I'll let you know." His dark gaze washed over her and Tara was captured in his spell. "Tara?"

"Yes?"

He clasped both her hands in his and pressed them to his chest. "Tell me you won't pledge your heart to someone else while I'm away."

She grinned warmly. "Never."

"Good." A smile graced his handsome face. "Then let's start making plans for the holidays. And about where you'd like to spend Christmas, in Savannah—or here."

"But, my dad—"

"I know. He's invited!"

"To Georgia?" she asked with pleased surprise. "Really?"

"Do you think he'd like my Granddad Lyle?" Heath shot her a cagey look and Tara giggled.

"Absolutely!"

"Then, we can talk about what might work best. We've got plenty of time between now and then. We can finalize our plans when I come back in December."

Tara was so overjoyed about spending Christmas with Heath that it was hard to think beyond the holiday. But she already was. Way deep in her heart, she was dreaming of more. She was imagining being with him always. "I can't wait to spend my first Christmas with you," she finally said.

"That makes two of us," he uttered, bringing his mouth to hers.

****

Heath felt like he was working a jigsaw puzzle with several missing pieces. Try as he might, he couldn't get cooperation from North Shore Central. And it was hard to aim straight when you were shooting in the dark. If Heath could get a handle on why they'd promoted Richard to begin with, he might propose a reasonable solution. The trick was, he couldn't inform North Shore Central that he had a personal interest at stake, and he could never let Richard know he'd had anything to do with saving his job. That was, if Heath was even able to accomplish that.

He raked a hand through his hair, thinking he'd never faced a bigger challenge. There was so much more than money involved; he had people's lives to think of. People he cared for. Heath hung his head in shame, wondering how many other families' well-beings he'd compromised, without ever fully understanding it. Tara and her dad were just one case. How many more had gone before, without Heath giving their situation a second thought?

That's when a stunning idea occurred. Heath knew what he wanted for Christmas, and it had nothing to do with himself. He wanted something better for Wellington International. He didn't want it to be the sort of institution that thrived based on other people's misery. He'd strive to make it a place that created safe havens for everyone. There were ways to finesse this. *Think smart.* So that nobody lost and everyone gained. Wellington International could do better than simply being a big business. It could also be a benevolent one.

Heath hadn't thought like this until he'd known Tara. She hadn't just altered his perspective; she'd changed his heart. And that heart had opened up to the reality that employees were facing. Across the country and around the world... If someone got displaced from one branch, couldn't Wellington International make a spot for them elsewhere? Might there be some sort of alternate institution? A charitable foundation where the laid-off workers could be employed, and in their own ways help to benefit others?

People like Richard could come on board. Folks with skills—like Richard had with carpentry.

Wellington International would pay these workers salaries, as they organized community efforts for the homeless...shut-ins, others in need... The pilot operation could begin in Savannah, then who knew where it could lead. Eventually, Heath could position a charitable arm in every location where there were Wellington banks. That way, it would be easy to transfer and reassign displaced workers, without any of them needing to relocate. The new ventures could be funded from a portion of the proceeds from any new acquisitions.

Heath's blood pumped harder as the ideas began formulating in his mind. He pressed his intercom button and called for Kristin. "Mind coming in here to take some notes?"

"Sure, boss,' she answered cheerily. "What are you planning?"

"How about changing the world?"

Chapter Seventeen

THE FOLLOWING WEEK, Tara was surprised to get a call from her dad asking her to meet him for coffee. He rarely took a break from the bank unless it was important. It wasn't even lunchtime, just after ten thirty, and Tara's workday had barely gotten started. She left Jeannie in charge of the shop, and asked Jeannie to give her regards to their regular Wednesday customer if Tara wasn't back in time to greet her. She entered the Moosejaw Mudhouse on Main Street, and spotted Richard sitting at a small table by himself.

Tara unwrapped her scarf and pulled off her gloves, taking a seat beside him. His brow was furrowed and his mouth creased in a frown. Tara reached out and gently touched his shoulder. "Dad? What's wrong?"

A swath of silvery hair swung forward as he ducked his chin. "I've been let go."

"Let go?" Tara couldn't imagine it. Hadn't he just been promoted at the end of last month? "I'm not sure I understand," she said. "Has something happened?"

Richard looked up with red-rimmed eyes. "Yeah, something's happened," he barked harshly. "Wellington International's what happened."

"What?"

He tightened his fingers around his paper coffee cup. "Why don't you ask your boyfriend about it?"

"Heath?" she asked, confounded. "But, what...?" Suddenly, Tara recalled how preoccupied he'd been, and how he'd said it had to do with bank business. Had Heath known about this in advance? Was he directly responsible for her father losing his job? She asked because she had to know. "North Shore Central's closing?"

"Being taken over by *big business*." Her dad sneered. "Just as I suspected all along. Can't trust 'em as far as you can throw 'em. And that includes that big-city beau of yours."

Tara swallowed hard, unwilling to believe it. "Why would they promote you if that's the case?"

Richard pursed his lips before answering. "One of their little tricks, I guess." He slowly shook his head.

"Only management's getting the shaft. We're being replaced by the Wellington team. The tellers, customer service reps, and admin folks are safe."

Tara sucked in a gasp. "You mean, if you hadn't been promoted—?"

"That's right," her dad said harshly. "I would have stayed. Not that I would have necessarily wanted to, given the unsavory nature of the takeover. Nobody heard anything about it until just this morning."

"Why today?"

"Folks are getting their two weeks' notice."

Tara ran the calculation in her head. "Two weeks before Christmas?" she asked in horror. "You can't mean it. Whose decision was this?"

"Probably a joint one," Richard said. "Or, maybe it's all on Wellington's head." He shrugged despairingly. "Who knows?"

Tara sagged in her chair, feeling the sting of moisture in her eyes. Had Heath really known this was coming, yet kept his mouth shut? Where was his sense of decency? Of charity? "I'm so sorry, Dad—"

She leaned toward him, but he gruffly nudged her away. "Not here. We're in public."

She eyed him sadly, her heart breaking for him.

"Going to keep my head held high," he continued. "I've already told my friends about my upgrade, and I'm not backing down on any of it. I'll stick with the new position until the bitter end. Which will come sooner rather than later," he added grimly.

"What will you do?" Tara asked, her voice cracking. Her dad was still in his fifties with lots of working years left, but job pickings were slim in this part of Maine. He'd been lucky to hold onto the position he'd had for so many years.

"I'll think of something," Richard replied, sounding totally unconvincing.

The shock and despair inside Tara began to turn into something else: hurt, anger…a sense of betrayal. Heath had to have known. He was the top man at Wellington International. He was bound to have to approve all the takeovers. What a fool she'd been, believing he was different. Thinking he was trustworthy and kind.

"We'll get through it. Somehow. Together." She reached for her dad's hand, but he pulled it away.

"And you and Heath?" he asked hoarsely. "Now, what's going to happen there?"

****

Tara had trouble focusing on her job for the rest of the day. When she told Jeannie what had happened, Jeannie couldn't believe it.

"He sounded like such a nice guy," she said with a frown.

"I know..." Tara's voice trembled, so she turned toward the register to disguise her quaking lower lip. Thankfully, they were experiencing a lull and no one else was in the shop. While Tara was always grateful for business, she couldn't have one of her customers see her fall apart, and she felt like she was about to at any minute.

When books sales had dropped off in October, at least she'd had her new love affair to distract her. When she'd been with Heath, anything had seemed possible. Restoring her business to top form...falling in love with a Savannah banker...building a bright future. Now, her lofty hopes and dreams had suddenly crashed and burned.

"How were November sales?" she asked Jeannie, looking for some good news to lift her spirits. Jeannie had been compiling the numbers for the past week and was supposed to be done this morning.

"I'm afraid not any better than October's, Tara." Jeannie's gray eyes glistened. "You know, I've been thinking...with our receipts being what they have been...maybe having two people working here full-time is too much of a stretch?"

Tara gaped at her. "Jeannie, no."

"I mean it, Tara," she said kindly. "I've already spoken with Dave. With us getting married in the spring, I could go part-time. We've been talking about starting a family right away, anyhow."

Tara clasped her hand. "I wouldn't do that to you. Once there's a baby coming, you might find you really need the hours. Children are expensive, and—"

"Tara," Jeannie said solemnly. "Just let me help you out a little. At least, say that you'll think it over."

If Tara was low before, she felt even more abysmal now. Her dad had been sacked, her boyfriend had betrayed her, the bookshop was failing, and she was about to cause her best friend on earth to partially lose her job. "You really are amazing," she said, hugging Jeannie tightly.

Jeannie returned her fierce hug then patted her back. "Everything will work out. You'll see."

"Sure," Tara said, though she couldn't in a million years see how.

****

By the time Heath called at eight o'clock, Tara had reached a boiling point. She'd gone from hurt to confused to dismayed—then furious, all in the course of one day. And, the emotions kept circling back around on themselves. Heath had texted when she was closing her shop to ask about calling later. When she hadn't replied, he must have assumed she'd simply never seen the text. She'd seen it all right, and had decided against issuing a few choice words in return. Those were better reserved for the telephone. For Tara had no intention of seeing Heath in person—ever again.

"Hey, how's it going?" he began in a cheerful tone.

"Not great."

"I'm sorry, Tara." She couldn't believe he had the nerve to sound sympathetic. "Bad day at the bookshop?"

"Bad day all around," she said flatly.

He hesitated a moment before asking, "Want to talk about it?"

She drew in a deep breath and released it, gathering her courage. "Not especially, but I will."

He waited in stunned silence while Tara sat weightily on the futon. At length, she questioned, "How long, Heath? How long have you known?" She hated to find her voice rising with emotion.

"About...?

She bit out the words. "North Shore Central."

"Something's happened, hasn't it?" he asked worriedly. "Your dad, Richard—?"

"He was fired today," she rushed in heatedly. "But you probably already knew that." She paused and gaped at the receiver. "Maybe you even *arranged* it."

"Tara, no... I would never—"

"Would never what, Heath?" she balked. "Lie to the woman you love? Deceive her father? *The man who welcomed you into his home?*"

"If you'd just slow down and let me explain—"

"You had to have known before then," she charged. "Before you came to Maine." Tara choked back a sob, thinking what a reckless fool she'd been. She thought she'd guarded her heart until precisely the right moment. Now, she saw her judgment in that department had failed miserably. "Did you?" she asked, her world tearing apart. "Did you, Heath? Did you know what was going to happen with North Shore Central...before you came here for Thanksgiving?" *And said you that loved me?* The notion was almost too painful to bear.

"I...well...yes, I did know about the North Shore Central acquisition, it's true." *Zing*. There it was: a red-hot flaming arrow straight through her heart. Tara clutched her free hand to her chest, her gut searing, as tears burned down her cheeks. "But Tara, it was so long ago. I mean, the deal was cut *months* before you and I met."

"But it was still on the table."

"Yeah, but I'd completely forgotten about it, to tell you the truth—"

"That's a fine turn of phrase for a man who wouldn't recognize the truth if he saw it."

"Careful, Tara. You're upset. You don't really know what you're saying."

Tara sniffed, roiling from his hurt and deception. "Don't I?"

"No, because you've yet to hear me out. If you'd only let me explain—"

"Will your explanation get my dad his job back?"

"At North Shore Central? No, probably not. But, I—"

"Then, I can't see what's left to discuss."

"How about us?" he asked hoarsely. "I was calling to ask about my plane tickets, and seeing you in mid-December?"

"I don't think that's such a hot idea."

"Okay, then. We can wait a while. Let things cool off first. You don't have to come to Savannah for Christmas. I'll come there—to you." His voice faltered unsurely. "If you'll have me?"

"And what kind of holiday do you imagine that would be?"

"I was hoping..." His voice shook noticeably. "...a white one?"

"Heath, I don't know what you're thinking, but this isn't going to work."

"But it can work! You don't understand. I've been doing everything in my power...trying like crazy to find a solution. And, I have!"

"Well, I'm afraid it's a little too late." Heath may have found a way to mend her tattered heart, but then he'd broken it apart again into a million tiny pieces. Tara's voice warbled the words catching in her throat. "I'm done with your *solutions*, Heath...and love...and stupid messages in a bottle."

"You don't mean it," he said, pleading. "You're not done with us?"

Tara couldn't see another way around it. Heath had broken her trust, and was ultimately responsible for causing her dad misery. How could she ever feel the same way about him? Tara couldn't believe she'd misread him so badly. In so doing, she'd made everything about her life worse.

She would have been so much better off if she'd never responded to his e-mail in the first place. But, she had, and now the only thing left to do in order to preserve her dignity—and her dad's—was cut things off. Tara had always believed herself strong and capable. But, even for her, this was too much. Her words broke apart as she said her farewell, stammering past her heartache.

"Goodbye, Heath. Have a...really nice... Christmas...in Savannah."

Then Tara clicked off her phone and cried her eyes out, her wails competing with the winds slamming the outside of her old barn building. She never should have been so trusting; she might have known. No good things come from taking chances. Rather than improve her life, she'd totaled it completely.

Tara felt very, very small and terribly cold, from the top of her head to the tips of her toes. She drew her knees up to her chest and wept some more, sobbing in fits and starts until her lungs heaved from the effort.

Tomorrow, she would do better. She'd pull herself together and devise some sort of plan, maybe a way to help her dad and save her bookshop. But tonight, she was way too overwhelmed and weary to consider it. All Tara wanted to do was curl into a ball and will the rest of the world away. Far, far away... And the place she wanted the most distance from was Savannah, Georgia.

Chapter Eighteen

"I'M SORRY, MAN," Byron said as they sat at the corner bar. "What are you going to do?"

Heath set his mug of beer down on the counter. "I thought I had a game plan, but she shot it down without even listening to me."

"You going to spend Christmas in Charlotte with your folks?"

"Nope. I think I'll just stick around here and take strolls down Tybee Beach."

"Now, that's maudlin."

"I'm thinking of putting in a petition to rename it." He quirked a sad smile Byron's way. "Heartbreak Shores, what do you think?"

"It will never fly."

"I hear Caroline's getting married."

"What? Already?" Byron blinked in shock. "To Will?"

"That's the word on the street."

"Which street?"

"Caroline's dog walker and my assistant, Kristin, are friends."

Byron shook his head. "Ouch. Talk about moving on."

"Yeah well, I did too." Heath pensively sipped from his beer. "I mean, I thought I had."

"I know. Sara and I believed you. She was already placing bets on the date of your wedding."

"My wedding?" Heath asked, surprised.

"She said you had *the look*." Byron raised both eyebrows. "The look of a man in love."

Heath heaved a sigh. "Well, maybe I was."

"I wouldn't go putting anything in the past tense," Byron cautioned.

"I hardly see the difference semantics make."

"It's all about attitude, Heath." Byron soundly patted his shoulder. "That can-do spirit!" Then he leaned toward Heath with a conspiratorial whisper. "What on earth happened to yours?"

****

Jeannie peered out the bookshop's front window in awe. A white van parked at the curb and a uniformed man holding a flower arrangement dashed through the snow to their door. "Another flower delivery! Wow! What's that make? The fourth one this week?"

Tara sighed in resignation. Heath had sent her a bouquet each day for the past eleven days, and would likely be sending another tomorrow. He'd sent them to her store during the week, and to her apartment over the weekend. There were so many vases competing with books for table and counter space in here, the place was beginning to look like a florist's shop rather than a bookstore.

"I know! This is crazy. I wish I could make him stop." The only thing was, that would mean Tara talking to him, and she was fully determined not to engage in discourse with Heath. If she did, she feared she might crumble, and fall into a heap of emotion again. Tara was finally getting herself together, and trying to see beyond what might have been.

She'd investigated a smaller rental space at a boutique that was closing near the bakery, and thought she might be able to convert it to a bookstore with some renovation work. Her dad had offered to help, and she insisted on paying him in return. They were still fighting over that, but Tara understood it was good for her father to have something concrete to look forward to in the lean days ahead. Jeannie and she had compromised on Jeannie cutting back her hours to seventy-five percent, and Jeannie said her fiancé, Dave, who was a builder, might have some contacts for Richard to pick up carpentry contracting work, if he was interested.

Tara was doing her best to construct a future far away from Heath, but he kept butting in—day after day—with a beautiful new bunch of flowers. Jeannie handed her the card that had come attached to the latest delivery, and Tara set the envelope down on the stack of others beside the cash register.

"Aren't you even going to open it?" Jeannie questioned. "I can't believe the curiosity's not killing you!"

It was, but Tara didn't want to get yanked back in like some helpless fish on a line. Not when she was finally making headway swimming on her own. If she reconciled with Heath, what would that say to her father? That his feelings didn't matter anymore? Tara couldn't do that to Richard. Not after he'd made so many sacrifices to raise her well. "I'll look at them later," she said glumly, not entirely sure when that would be.

Jeannie gazed around the fragrant room at the colorful flower displays. "What are you going to do with these?"

"I thought I'd drop them by the retirement home after we close on Christmas Eve."

Jeannie clasped her hands together, pleased. "What a beautiful thought. I know the residents will appreciate them."

"Yeah." For a melancholy moment, Tara thought of Lyle. That made her think of Savannah, and Heath. She choked back a sob and pretended to be fussing with a cardboard stand exhibiting new book arrivals, but Jeannie read her.

"It's okay to change your mind, you know?" she said softly. "Christmas is the season for forgiving."

"Some things are easier to forgive than others," Tara said weakly.

Jeannie frowned in understanding. "I know."

"So will you help me?" Tara asked, changing the subject. "Help me donate this ridiculous mess of flowers to a good cause? Your car is bigger than mine. I thought between the two of us...?"

Jeannie beamed brightly. "You know I will."

****

After making the retirement home flower delivery on Christmas Eve, Tara returned to her shop to lock things up for the holiday. She told Jeannie she had a few final receipts to run in order to close out the books, but the truth was Tara simply wanted to be alone with her thoughts before meeting her dad for seven o'clock church. They'd planned to attend the service together and then have chili at her place. The next day, she'd have Christmas dinner at her dad's house, as always. Though, given all that had happened this month, their celebration promised to be a little less cheery than in years past.

Tara walked morosely around her store, thinking how much she was going to miss it. The amply sized rooms in the old house had high ceilings, and a large open area near the entrance, which served as the storefront. Two smaller rooms in the back, which had once functioned as bedrooms, were now dedicated reading areas with comfy couches and chairs. Jeannie always kept coffee going on a table in one of them, and typically brought in fresh baked goods to share. Tara enjoyed running the kind of store where people didn't just shop—they lingered. Because it was a warm, friendly space dedicated to such high ideals: romance and love.

She paused by the register, eying the stack of cards from Heath, and her heart sank. He obviously was sorry for what he'd done, but—in this case—could sorry be enough? Just look at her dad and the unwelcomed changes to his life this bank takeover would bring. And, one of the worst parts about it was the way Heath had deceived her. If only he'd told her the truth from the beginning...

Tara's face flushed hot when she realized where that would have led. If Heath had let on about Wellington International's acquisition sooner, she likely would have cut their relationship off then. Perhaps that would have been better. That way, Tara wouldn't have been made to suffer so much. Just looking around this empty room and recalling the number of flowers that had been here, Tara understood that Heath was hurting, as well. He clearly wouldn't have gone to so much trouble, if he wasn't equally devastated by their breakup. Unless this was simply an ego thing, and Heath was the sort of man who couldn't stand it when he didn't win.

Tara recalled the tender look in Heath's eyes the moment he'd first told her he loved her, and found it hard to believe him capable of being so calculating. And yet, he *had* calculated. He'd made a conscious choice not to inform her, or her father, about what was going to happen to North Shore Central. Even if Heath couldn't have changed the outcome, he might have done the humane thing by trying to prepare her, and most especially her father, for the inevitable.

She sighed heavily and sat on the stool behind the counter, recalling Jeannie's words. Perhaps Christmas was a time of charity, but she wasn't quite sure she could muster any for Heath. There was one thing she could bring herself to do at least. She'd read through his cards.

Chapter Nineteen

"WHAT'S WRONG, CHILD? My Christmas ham's no good this year?"

Tara poked disconsolately at her food, feeling a heavy weight in her stomach. She was anything but hungry. In fact her throat seemed swollen shut. She tried to force a small swallow of water down it, struggling with the effort. "I'm sorry, Dad. I just don't have much of an appetite today."

"This is about that banker, isn't it? Heath Wellington?"

"I'm so sorry about what he did to you," she said, her voice cracking. "It was awful, unforgive—"

"Wasn't him," Richard said, taking a forkful of scalloped potatoes.

"What?"

"Found out through the grapevine that old man Tucker helped orchestrate the whole thing."

"Mr. Tucker? But, why? Wasn't he the branch manager be—?" Tara's words fell off as she put the scenario together. She gaped in incredulity. "You mean, he stepped down on purpose and let you take his job, because he knew the existing management was being replaced?"

"Sly as a fox, that one," Richard said, gesturing with his fork. "A crooked one, that is."

"What a horrible, self-serving—"

"I know, lass. But what's a man to do?" Her dad shrugged halfheartedly. "I've decided I'm better off without those Wellington people." He set down his fork to study her. "But now...I'm not so sure about *you*."

"What on earth are you talking about?" Tara asked, perplexed.

"That ex-fellow of yours called me."

He didn't. Couldn't have... "Heath?" Tara asked, aghast. "And you took the call?"

"I at least gave the man a listen," Richard responded. "Which was apparently more than you were willing to do."

Tara's head spun from this turn of events. Heath had talked to her dad? *When? Why?*

"I told him not to worry too much about it. That's how you are: headstrong. Your mother was like that, too. Never listened to a word I said." He slowly lifted his wineglass. "I suppose I wasn't too great at listening, either."

Tara was stunned by her dad's mention of his former wife, since he seldom brought her up in conversation. He went on, "Heath got me thinking about Sophia and what went wrong, all that time ago."

She sat there in shocked silence as he continued.

"I always blamed her for leaving me, you know that."

"It was *us*, Dad. She left both of us."

"Yes, and that part was wrong." He fondly patted Tara's hand. "A parent should never abandon a child, but your mom, you see, wasn't much more than a child herself. Only twenty-three. You were two years old, so you barely knew her, and that's too bad. She was a fiery woman, she was. Beautiful to look at and with a very strong spirit."

Tara swallowed past the lump in her throat.

"You look a lot like her, you know." His dark eyes glistened. "I like to think you got all the best parts, of me and Sophia together. But it seems you got a negative aspect, too. Stubbornness."

"Dad—"

He raised his hand to stop her. "I'm not trying to admonish you as much as myself. What I'm saying is that I started thinking about Sophia, and how she left. In some ways I think she wanted me to go after her, but I didn't."

His forthrightness touched Tara to her soul. "Why not?" she asked softly.

Richard hung his head in shame. "I suppose I was afraid. Scared she would reject me a second time. But, in looking back, I'm not so sure that she would have. She wanted me to stand up for us, and to fight for the love we had. Because—I've never told you this, Tara, but it's true—Sophia and I did have it. We loved each other deeply once upon a time."

"What happened?"

"I became preoccupied with work, I suppose. Spent more time reading the paper than holding her hand. She was tired after long days of being a housewife, and, at a very young age, I became a grouchy old man. I'm not proud of that, and I've never admitted it to anyone until now. I've only recently admitted it to myself. But, when your mother left, it wasn't entirely her fault. I was partially to blame."

He reached out and latched onto Tara's arm. "But not for her leaving you, child. She should never have done that. Yet, her mistake has been my greatest blessing."

Tara felt moisture on her cheeks and she realized she was crying. "Thanks, Dad. You've been a blessing to me, too. I never could have made it without you."

"No," he said tenderly. "But I think now my turn is done." He folded his napkin and set it down on the table.

"What are you saying?"

"Don't let something good get away from you just because you're afraid... In this life, you have to work for the things that are worth holding onto. You can't expect them to come easy."

Heat burned in Tara's eyes.

"Heath said he sent you flowers and more than a dozen notes." His face was awash with compassion as his brow rose. "Did you read any of them?"

Tara nodded numbly, because she had read them all, and she'd cherished every word. She hadn't wanted her heart to open back up, but it had...little by little, like a rosebud blooming beneath the sun. Heath had profusely apologized and professed his love. He'd also done something else. He'd begged her to give him one more chance.

"What did he say?"

"He asked me to meet him halfway."

"That wasn't figurative, I suspect. He meant in New York City."

She sucked in a breath. "Heath told you?"

"He only said where, not when?"

"Today at five o'clock."

Richard checked his watch, seeing it was just after one.

"Well? What are ya waiting for, lass? You'd better get a move on!"

Tara's pulse pounded, as heat flooded her face. She'd be a fool to let Heath get away, and she knew it. He'd tried over and over again to make amends and Tara had selfishly turned a deaf ear. It took two to make a relationship work, but only one to sustain a fight.

She'd let her pride and her pigheadedness blind her to the fact that Heath really loved her, and that there might be more to his story than she believed. Given what they'd had, and everything she'd felt for Heath, didn't Tara at least owe him the chance to explain? She stared worriedly at her father, fearing it might already be too late.

"Even if I left right now, I'd never make it in time. I don't have airline reservations."

Richard's dark eyes sparkled. "My friend Martin has a private plane."

Tara knew Martin didn't own it; he piloted it for a wealthy Boston family with a vacation home in Beaumont. "It's not his plane, Dad."

"No, but he asked the missus and she said of course he could borrow it for such an important mission. As long as he pays for the petrol... I offered to cover it with money from my savings. And, Martin is on standby, just waiting for my call." Richard grinned warmly. "Merry Christmas, sweetheart."

Tara leapt to her feet and hugged him. "You did all that for me? But why?"

Richard patted the arms she'd looped around his neck. "Because, my girl, I love you more than life itself." Then he added with a wink, "And I've got a suspicion that a certain Savannah banker loves you, too."

Tara now trusted implicitly that Heath did. What's more, she held the certain conviction that she loved Heath back—with her whole heart. There had to be a way to compromise! Isn't that what Heath was asking her to do? Meet him in the middle? Accept his gesture by extending her hand?

There was obviously more to the bank deal than she grasped. If her father could be reasonable about understanding, then she should be, too. She couldn't wait to see Heath and hear what he had to say. But mostly, she ached to wrap her arms around him and apologize.

Tara stood abruptly, bringing a hand to her forehead. "Oh my gosh! I don't have a thing to wear!"

Her dad surveyed her jeans, sweater, and boots. "What you've got on looks just fine!"

Tara's nerves were on edge and her heart raced wildly, but yes, she wanted to do it. She was ready to take this chance and see where it went. She stared back at her father, uncertainly, waiting for him to change his mind.

Instead, he prodded her along with a push of his hands. "Go! Go! I'll call Martin when you leave. He said he'd meet you at the airfield. And, don't forget your coat!" he called, when she was nearly to the door.

"What about the snow?"

"Lucky for you, there's been a break in the storm." Richard's dark eyes twinkled. "Seems like Santa is on your side."

Chapter Twenty

HEATH STOOD AT the Manhattan entrance to the Brooklyn Bridge as winds ripped across the water. It was a pretty time of day and foot traffic was heavier than he expected, with large groups of pedestrians out for holiday strolls. A heavy mist lifted off the East River as evening fell and twinkling city lights illuminated the night sky. The views of both Brooklyn and Manhattan were stunning with the Statue of Liberty lording over the landscape. Heath hoped he hadn't made a mistake in issuing an ultimatum. Then again, he'd have to man up and face the music sometime. If he didn't hear from Tara today, that meant things were over. He'd promised to never contact her again.

Since she hadn't replied to any of his voicemails or text messages, and had completely ignored his flower deliveries, Heath had a hard time remaining optimistic. Yet, Richard—of all people—had urged him not to give up trying. The last person on earth Heath

had anticipated as an ally was Tara's father. The older
man had warmed to Heath once he understood Heath's
intentions were sincere. Remarkably, he'd also believed
Heath about the bank takeover situation, and said he
was mature enough not to take things personally.

When Heath had filled Richard in on his plans
for developing a charitable organization run by
displaced bank workers, Richard had become even
more animated. He liked people who could think on
their feet, and appreciated that Heath didn't accept the
status quo—he looked for innovative solutions. Richard
was particularly intrigued by Heath's proposal that
Richard move to Savannah to help spearhead the new
project. He'd be in management then for sure. Richard
also claimed he'd long been interested in moving to a
southern climate, but that he'd never been able to
consider it out of fear of abandoning Tara.

Heath anxiously checked his watch again,
seeing it was five minutes past the hour. Perhaps Tara
was running late, or her train—or cab—had been
delayed. He shifted on his feet, bracing himself against
the cold. It was below freezing tonight and predicted to
snow soon.

He'd booked hotel rooms for him and Tara at
the same place where they'd stayed when they'd first

met, and he was hoping they'd get to stay there again. Winds gusted and Heath shivered, thinking he really didn't know what to expect. Mostly, he just hoped that Tara would show. Heath had a plan, of course. But, just like during their very first date, so much depended on Tara to set their course.

****

Tara raced up the stone staircase leading to the Brooklyn Bridge. Since Heath had said to meet him at the entrance, she didn't want to stray too far away. Chilly winds tore off the East River, but the cheery pedestrians crossing the bridge scarcely seemed to notice. Some traveled in large groups, others in pairs, pausing periodically to snap photos, or marvel at the number of padlocks previous passersby had attached to the bridge's various abutments and suspension wires, as a way of memorializing their visit or perhaps paying tribute to somebody special.

She scanned the crowd, but there was no one resembling Heath in sight. With his solid build and that easy gait, she'd recognize him in an instant. Tara caught her breath and checked the time on her phone, seeing it was seven minutes past the hour. Surely, he would have waited at least ten minutes past five, anticipating her arrival? Her heart beat harder and her panic increased. What if he didn't wait? What if he thought she'd stood him up, and had taken off?

No, that didn't make sense, Tara reasoned. Heath was a seasoned business professional, accustomed to waiting things out.

He'd grant me at least fifteen minutes...

Sweat beaded her brow.

Wouldn't he?

Maybe she was merely being paranoid, and Heath was the one running late. Yes, that could be it exactly.

Tara held on to that hope until five-fifteen.

****

Heath's spirits plummeted as the minutes ticked on. Perhaps he'd been deluded to think Tara would meet him here. Maybe it was his fault for not paying for her ticket? But, no, that couldn't be it. He had to believe that Tara would come of her own accord. That she would deem the journey worth it. For he did, with his entire heart and soul, and he'd laid them both on the line. Heath began to pace back and forth by the bridge entryway.

He could call, but she might not answer.

Text, but she wouldn't reply.

His phone buzzed in his coat pocket and Heath's heart stilled. He couldn't bear to hope...was scared to look...but he had to, willing it was her with every fiber of his being.

Where are you?

It was a text from Tara!

Heath drew in a deep breath and replied quickly.

Here! On the Brooklyn Bridge.

An alert sounded seconds later.

I can't see you?

Heath anxiously glanced around, surveying the individual faces. He couldn't see Tara, either.

Where are you?

On the bridge! In Brooklyn!

Brooklyn? In that split second Heath knew.
Tara was on the opposite end of the bridge. When he'd
said to meet him on the Brooklyn Bridge, she must
have assumed he'd meant on that city's side.

I'm in Manhattan.

Heath berated himself for his tactical error in
not giving clearer instructions. There was only one
thing to do. He rapidly texted again and apparently
Tara must have done the same. Her identical message
crossed airspace with his.

Meet me in the middle!

****

Tara's boots left the pavement the instant she
got his text. Heath was less than a mile away! She
darted forward, pressing her way through the crowd.
Tara had never been much of a runner, but this was the

marathon of her life. Her destiny waited just two track lengths ahead.

If Heath met her halfway, he'd cover the same distance in no time. Tara ran with all her might, feeling fire in her veins as icy air stung her face. The wintry cold had no hold on her now. The only one she wanted to hold her was Heath.

****

Heath raced through the bitter chill with one thought in mind. Tara would be in his arms soon. Whatever had gone wrong, no matter what mistakes he'd made, he'd fix them, if she'd only agree to be his. Heath picked up his pace, his shoes pounding the walking path beneath him. When he saw Tara rushing in his direction, his spirit soared.

Tara's pretty green eyes lit up and a smile warmed her lips. "Heath!" she called loudly. "Over here!" Her arms were up and waving as she barreled toward him, weaving in and out of curious onlookers who began to peel off to the side.

"Tara!" he cried, the word scraping from his throat. He'd never been happier to see anyone in his life. The pedestrians on his portion of the bridge slowed to a stall, as well. Soon, everyone around them had stopped to watch the impromptu reunion between the apparently estranged lovers.

She tore toward him and leapt into his arms. Heath caught Tara joyfully, swinging her around and around. "I was so afraid you wouldn't come," he said huskily.

Her voice quaked as she gazed up at him. "I thought when you said the Brooklyn—"

"I know, darling. I know. It's *totally* my fault."

She eyed him longingly. "The important thing is we're here." A wave of relief crashed over him. This was his chance. Heath gently set her down, and spoke from the heart.

"I want to apologize, Tara. For any of the hurt and confusion I caused you, and your dad."

Her eyes glistened. "Heath, I'm sorry too. So, so sorry...I wouldn't listen to you."

"I've made some mistakes, but please believe they were done out of wrongheadedness—not malice."

She nodded thoughtfully, like she understood, though her face was flushed.

Heath brought his arms around her, embracing her fully. "I'll make it up to you—to you and your dad, both." He viewed her convincingly. "I have a plan."

She smiled and her lips trembled. "There's no better planner than you."

That was all the encouragement Heath needed to make his next move. He astonished her by pulling a small velvet ring box from his coat pocket.

At that precise moment, it began to snow.

People all around them *ooh*ed and *ahh*ed, as tears pooled in Tara's beautiful green eyes.

"I know I've made a mess of this. But if you'll give me the rest of our lifetimes, I'll make it right."

He flipped open the ring box, exposing a gorgeous two-carat solitaire. It was set in an intricate white gold setting, which had been meticulously designed for Juliette by Lyle. Little rosebud flowerets sat at the base of the stone, which glittered like new-fallen snow.

Heath had used the original setting, but upgraded the diamond for Tara. He'd taken a risk in having this custom-made piece of jewelry altered, but from the look on Tara's face it was paying off in spades.

"This engagement ring belonged to my Grandma Juliette," he told her. "She and my Granddad Lyle were married for over sixty years. I'm hoping we'll be that lucky."

Tara gaped in surprise as tears streamed down her cheeks. "Are you...?"

Heath took her hand and dropped down on one knee to stunned gasps from the crowd. "Tara McAdams," he rasped hoarsely. "Will you marry me?"

She clamped a hand over her mouth, but she was nodding. And crying. Boy, was she crying—to beat the band. But those were joyful tears, Heath was sure of it.

"You bet I will!" she said, tugging him to his feet. He motioned toward her left hand and Tara quickly removed her glove, allowing Heath to slip the ring on her finger.

"I had it adjusted for you," he said. "It's a perfect size six."

She stared up at him and her face held a beautiful blush. "It's marvelous. The most incredible ring I've ever seen."

"I was hoping that, after the wedding, we could honeymoon in Ireland?"

Tara sighed happily. "Ireland?"

"You said you've always wanted to go." Heath observed her lovingly. "And, sweetheart, I'll go anywhere with you."

She grinned, then asked jauntily, "I suppose you'll be asking me to move to Savannah, next?"

"I'd be so honored if you would. I've got my business there and my granddad—"

"What about my bookshop?" she cut in, but she was beaming even more brightly than before.

"Do you think that Jeannie might be interested in taking over the original Happy Hearts? A really awesome rental space has just opened up around the corner from Forsyth Park, and I was wondering if you might like to start a second store? With a certain investor's help, of course," he added with a twinkle.

Tara's gaze sparkled merrily. "Heath Wellington, I think that's a fine idea!" She stopped suddenly...worry furrowing her brow. "And, my dad?"

Heath grinned, surprising her with his answer. "Richard tells me he's ready for warmer weather."

Tara blinked like she couldn't believe it. "Well, then! I suppose it's all settled."

Heath took her back in his arms. "So, what do you say?" he pleaded warmly, as snow continued to pound them. "Will you move to Savannah, and be my bride?"

A woman in the crowd yelled, "*Yes!* Say *yes!*" and Tara laughed out loud. "Sounds like I'd better agree with her, or the mob will come after me."

It was Heath's turn to laugh, and his spirit was light. So light, he felt he could fly. Tara and he were going to build an amazing life together in Georgia. More amazing than he'd ever dreamed possible. "I think you've just made me the happiest man alive."

"You've made me unbelievably happy, too." She paused, then petitioned boldly, "But you *will* still explain...? About my dad's bank, and why you didn't—?"

Heath pulled her closer. "Yes, darling. *Everything.*"

Her hat and wavy dark tresses were dusted white, but her cheeks burned bright pink. Love and affection were written in her eyes. "You're what I wanted for Christmas, Heath."

Heath cupped her face in his hands and heat flooded his veins. He'd never adored a woman so fervently or wanted anyone in his life this much. "You're what I want *always*, Tara."

She nodded sweetly as his mouth moved in, and snowflakes gently danced around them. "I'm yours."

"Together forever through time," Heath whispered. "Lyle had that engraved in your engagement ring for Juliette. Now, it's etched in my heart."

"That's beautiful."

His lips brushed over hers. "So are you."

Heath kissed her soundly while wintry winds blew, ruffling their coats and riffling their hair. Then, to cheers and applause from their onlookers, Heath scooped Tara up in his arms and carried her all...the...way...back to Manhattan, where they would plan the rest of their future together, starting with a romantic dinner for two at an upscale restaurant tonight.

The End

Author Bio

NEW YORK TIMES and *USA Today* bestselling author Ginny Baird has published novels in print and online and received screenplay options from Hollywood for her family and romantic comedy scripts. Whether writing lighthearted romantic comedy or spine-tingling romantic suspense, she delights in delivering heartwarming stories. Ginny is the author of the Christmas Town series, the Holiday Brides series, the Summer Grooms series, a Romantic Ghost Stories series, and several standalone books. She invites you to visit her website and connect with her on social media. http://www.ginnybairdromance.com/